A DEAD GIVEAWAY

by Emsworth writer
Simon Hawke

Copies available on Amazon & Kindle

Chapter 1

Ever wondered why some people rub you up the wrong way the first time you meet them? There you are, sitting minding your own business, when someone comes up to you and says,

'Hello, Joey. I'd like you to meet so-and-so.'

What they're really saying is they've been lumbered with this so-and-so character and they want to load him off on you. Which usually means only one thing. So-and-so's a wally.

Teachers are real experts at it. Don't believe me? Well, just watch next time you get some new kid starting in your class.

'Now, guys. I'd like you all to meet Anthony. Anthony's joining us as from today and I want you to make him feel really welcome. Anthony, you can sit over there next to Joey.'

Which is just fine - unless your name happens to be Joey and there's an empty desk next to yours. First thing you know, the kid's following you round like he's on a piece of elastic. And the questions! When does the bell go for lunch, Joey? Which floor's the Music Room on, Joey? Where's the secretary's office, Joey? It gets so that by the time three-thirty comes round, you feel like the trivial pursuits champion of the education world.

So you're standing there by the gate, waiting for that fit little piece with the dark hair in Year 8, when who should come along?

You guessed it.

'Sir said you live near me, Joey. He said you'd show me the short cut through the park.'

See what I mean? You've been lumbered. Happens all the time. It even happened to me once.

Mind you, it wasn't a teacher who lumbered me. Leastways, not directly. No, it was my sister. Her name's Vicki, and as usual she had to get our Mam to help her 'cos she'd never have managed it on her own.

Vicki's a couple of years older than me, and she thinks she's clever. All on account of she got a place at this snobby girls' school the other side of town where everyone calls her Victoria.

Actually, the fact that it was our Vicki who lumbered me didn't really matter at the time. I was more concerned with what - or rather, who - she lumbered me with.

Jean was his name.

And he was a Froggy - you know, from France, the cobbled end of the Channel Tunnel. Where they've got Paris and the Eiffel Tower and that. 'Cept that this particular Froggy didn't come from Paris. He came from Longville.

No, I'd never heard of it either, but he said it was near St. Tropez. Now, I had heard of that on account of it being where they can sunbathe on the beach in the nudgie 'cos the sun's so hot all the time.

You don't get much call for that sort of thing round here. More's the pity. Sure, we get the sun now and again, but the tide doesn't come in as far as Birmingham which means we're a bit short on beaches. Best we can manage is some sand in the jump pit over the local park. We go there sometimes if it's nice, but I've never seen anybody sunbathing in the nudgie. Don't suppose the parkie would like it much anyway. He throws a wobbly if you so much as walk on his precious grass - and that's with all your clothes on!

I asked Jean about this St. Tropez place once. He said he'd only been there a couple of times and that was when he was younger, and no, he hadn't taken any photos of people sunbathing in the nudgie. He did have a picture in his wallet of his pet rabbit if I wanted to see it. I said, 'Nah, forget it,' 'cos it didn't seem quite the same somehow.

    Not that I want you to get the impression it was always like that between Jean and me - you know, chatting and sort of friendly like.

    'Cos it wasn't.

    Leastways, not at the beginning.

Chapter 2

Looking back now, I suppose you could say he caught me at a bad time, arriving like that right in the middle of 'Blue Peter' on Cbeebies.

To be fair, it wasn't really his fault. I mean, he'd only been in the country a few hours so you could hardly expect him to know when 'Blue Peter' was on. Mrs Lewis should have known though, her being a teacher an' all.

It was Mrs Lewis who brought Jean round in her car. She brought our Vicki, too, on account of Victoria's in her class and Mrs Lewis said she wanted to apologise for keeping her so late after school.

I said there was no need to apologise and that she could keep our Vicki all night if she wanted. Then our Mam gave me one of her looks and I shut up.

Besides, they were just about to announce the winners of the poetry competition on 'Blue Peter' and I wanted to hear all about the prize I was going to win. Two tickets for a return trip on a cross-Channel ferry. That would mean I'd get to see the sea.

My mate Mohammed Sharif – we call

him Little Mo on account of he's from India and a bit on the short side – well, he reckoned as the trip might be overnight and I wouldn't get to see much in the dark. But that was only 'cos he was jealous when I said he couldn't have the spare ticket. Little Mo's the sort who gets sea-sick in the bath, and I didn't think it'd look good on Cbeebies having one of the prize-winners throwing up over the side.

Actually, what I didn't tell Mo at the time was that I'd already promised the spare ticket to the fit little piece with the dark hair out of Year 8.

Sharon's her name. She'd never been to the sea either and she got all excited when I told her, and I let her give me a kiss. Then she went quiet again and said as how her Dad probably wouldn't let her go. Said he'd had this thing about the sea ever since her Mum had up and run away with a sailor from the 'Ark Royal'.

I said as how I reckoned her Dad was having her on. Everyone knew the 'Ark Royal' was an aircraft carrier before it was scrapped and anyway it couldn't get all the way up to Birmingham. There were too many locks on the canal.

Sharon thought for a bit, and then said

as how she could tell her Dad she was going on a school trip to Dudley Zoo. Said that's what she always told him when she didn't want him to know where she was really going.

I said I thought it was a bit risky, but she laughed and I let her give me another kiss 'cos she'd seemed to like the first one.

I had to hand it to Sharon. She had it all worked out. Apparently, every time she was supposed to be at the Zoo, she'd nip into Cardfactory or somewhere and buy one of those postcards with a picture of an animal on it. Then she'd give the card to her Dad just to prove where she'd been.

'He pins them up on his bedroom wall,' she said. 'You know, like a big game hunter. He's got almost a full set – lions, tigers, elephants, the lot. Last time, he asked me to check out if the zoo had any killer whales but the lady in Smiths said she didn't think they did postcards of killer whales. So I had to settle for one with some tropical fish on.'

'Didn't he mind?' I said.

'No,' she said. 'It was in black and white so I told him they were baby killer whales that hadn't growed up yet. Dead chuffed he was an' all.'

Well, after that, I couldn't let her down,

could I? Not if she was willing to go to all that trouble just so's we could see the sea and have a trip on a ferry. So I went straight round to Little Mo's to borrow this book I knew he had, and that night I wrote this ace poem all about ships and the sea and that. I sent it off first post the next day.

So, then, there I was sitting on the floor in front of the telly, waiting for the presenter, the one with the funny hair-cut and the dog, to read my name out, when in walks our Mam with Vicki and our Vicki's teacher and this Jean character.

I wouldn't have minded, but this Mrs Lewis woman starts yapping on dead loud like she's giving an assembly or something. Next thing I know, our Mam's fiddling with the remote control and shouting that she can't hear herself think with all the racket going on. I thought she was meaning Mrs Lewis, so it was a few seconds before I sussed. Even then I couldn't believe it.

It was like one of those nightmares you get after reading too many vampire books. There's this bloke standing in front of the cameras with what had to be my poem in his hand, telling thousands of people all over the country that yours truly had won first prize in the poetry competition – and what do I get?

Some woman I've never seen before babbling on about this Jean kid and what a dreadful mistake there's been. And all the time the bloke's mouth is doing an imitation of a goldfish on account of our Mam's turned the sound off!

By the time I'd got across the floor and put the sound up again real loud, they were playing the signature tune and that was that.

Well, someone was going to pay, I can tell you. And you didn't have to be boffin of the week to work out who exactly.

I suppose you're wondering why I didn't leg it straight round to one of my mates' houses, or to Sharon's, just to check I had won the trip on the ferry after all.

Well, it wasn't quite as easy as that.

You see, there aren't many kids I know who watch telly that time of day, and specially not Cbeebies and 'Blue Peter'. As for Sharon, well, she hasn't had a telly since that time the cops came round and said as how the one she did have was nicked, and her dad had to go to court for receiving stolen property. Hundred pounds they fined him an' all. Which was a bit steep 'cos according to Sharon the bloke in the pub where he'd bought it said it was probably only worth twenty-five and he'd let Sharon's dad have it for twenty.

Not that it would have made much difference anyway. 'Cos you see, there's one important detail about the competition that I haven't told you yet.

Don't get me wrong. I did write a poem about the sea and that, and I did send it off. And I included a stamped addressed envelope so's they could send me the tickets and details of how to get Sharon and me to wherever the ferry was. Only I didn't use my proper name – not my real name anyway.

I used one of those funny names that famous writers make up when they don't want people to know who wrote their books.

Pseudonyms they're called.

I got the idea from Miss Shepherd, our English teacher. She was talking about the time when women writers had to use fellas' names otherwise people wouldn't read their books.

Not that I was thinking about being popular when I put this other name on the poem. I was thinking more about self-preservation on account of writing poems and sending them in to 'Blue Peter' isn't quite how most kids round here spend their time.

So that's why I didn't tell anyone about the poem. 'Cept Sharon, of course. Oh, and Little Mo.

I hadn't wanted to tell Mo, but it was the only way I could get to borrow this book he had. Little Mo has loads of books 'cos his Mam works part-time in the library and she gets them cheap when they're too tatty to put back on the shelves.

'Seas and Oceans of the World', said Little Mo, flicking through the pages. 'What do you want this for?'

'I want to look at the pictures,' I said.

'What do you want to look at the pictures for?' he said.

''Cos I've got to write a poem about the sea and I need some ideas and if you tell anybody I'll fight on you, Mo Sharif,' I said.

'What you got to write a poem about the sea for?' said little Mo.

So I told him. About the competition and taking Sharon to see the sea and about the trip on a ferry. Mind you, I didn't tell him everything. Like I didn't tell him about putting a different name on the poem so's no-one would know it was really me as wrote it.

'Never met anyone who's into writing poems before,' said Little Mo. 'Not the sort of thing people do round here, is it?'

'No,' I said.

'Worse than being a boffin that is, writing poems,' he said quietly.

'S'pose it is,' I said, slipping the book into the bottom of the sports bag I'd been careful to bring along for the purpose. I knew what he was getting at. I could count on Mo not to let on to anyone else about the poem and that.

'Ta, Mo,' I said as he was letting me out. 'And don't worry. I can look after meself.'

I could, too. Been doing it for years.

But that was before Jean showed up on the scene.

Chapter 3

By rights, he shouldn't have showed up at all. In fact, according to Mrs Lewis, he shouldn't even have been in the country.

She showed our Mam the list. There were twenty names on it. Ten boys and ten girls and a neat little tick beside each name.

'I've been arranging these exchange trips for years,' I heard her saying, 'and not once have I ever had anything like this happen. Twenty. We always arrange to take twenty. And then twenty of our young ladies make a return visit the following term. You can't imagine the shock, Mrs Edwards. Arriving at the station and suddenly finding you have twenty-one dear little souls waiting for you when all along you've been expecting twenty. Distressing, most distressing.'

All the time this was going on, our Mam was nodding her head and trying to look sympathetic. What with that, and Mrs Lewis, and then our Vicki looking like it was her birthday and Christmas rolled into one, something told me I wasn't going to like where all this was leading to.

And I didn't.

The gist of it was that Mrs Lewis had added ten and ten and come up with vingt-et-un. Which meant, of course, that one of her dear little souls had nowhere to stay for the next week or so.

Jean was the 'et-un'.

Me, I couldn't see what all the fuss was about.

Can of Coke, packet of crisps, back to the ferry port, and with a following wind he could've been home in time for supper. Mrs Lewis had other ideas.

'I know it's terribly short notice, Mrs Edwards,' I heard her saying in that voice teachers always put on when they want you to do something for them. 'But Victoria said she was sure you wouldn't mind, and I really would be most awfully grateful. You would, of course, be fully reimbursed for any additional expenditure for board and keep and excursions and that sort of thing.'

At that point, the only excursion I had in mind for the kid was a one-way, no expenses trip out through the front door.

If only our Mam had come right out with it first time, everything would have been fine. Even teachers understand the word 'No' if it's said with feeling. They should do – they use it often enough.

Only our Mam didn't say no. She didn't say yes either, not straightaway that is. But as soon as she opened her mouth I knew it was only a matter of time.

'Well, I'd like to help, of course, Mrs Lewis, but you see, it's a bit awkward. I mean, there's only the bedrooms for the three of us like, and I don't really see how …'

It was pathetic. I almost felt sorry for her the way Mrs Lewis poo-pooed all her excuses like she was some sort of over-grown schoolgirl.

And our Vicki didn't exactly help matters.

Specially when she said as how this Jean character could move in with me!

'Our Joey's room's plenty big enough,' she said in that sickly butter-wouldn't-melt sort of way she puts on.

'So's the Aston Expressway,' I growled. 'Why don't you go and lie down on it? Bit of luck, you might get run over and then he can have your room.'

At least the Froggy kid thought it was funny, even if our Vicki didn't. I saw him sort of smiling quietly to himself, like as if he didn't want the others to notice. Which they didn't, of course. Our Mam and Mrs Lewis were too busy sorting out what the kid was and wasn't supposed to do while he was with us.

I didn't catch all of it on account of Mrs

Lewis started whispering things to our Mam which made it difficult to cop a proper earful. Surprised me that, her being a teacher an' all. You'd have thought she'd have had more manners.

    Not that it made much difference. The Froggy, it seemed, was here to stay – for a week at least.

    Started me thinking, that did. I mean, he'd only been in the country a matter of hours, and already he had two grown women and our Vicki eating out of his hand. What was it with him? I glanced across to where he was standing all innocent-like by the doorway. About my age - maybe a year older – tall, dark hair, sun tan, bit of a flashy dresser … The penny began to drop.

    He saw me staring, and grinned. You'd have sworn he'd polished his teeth specially for the occasion. I stared back, blowing the biggest bubble I could with my bubble-gum and waited for it to burst.

    'Creep!' I thought.

Chapter 4

It was break-time Friday morning before I met up with Little Mo again. Thursday he'd been away from school on some art trip or other. I reckoned there was just a chance he might have watched 'Blue Peter'.

He had, too.

'See you didn't win, then,' he said. 'Not even one of them runners'-up badges.'

I told him about Mrs Lewis and the Froggy kid and about our Mam and how she'd switched the sound off so's I couldn't hear the prizewinners being read out.

'Wouldn't have made no difference,' he said. 'I listened out specially. Went through the whole list they did. Not a Joey or an Edwards amongst the lot of them.'

He didn't know about me using one of those funny pseudonym names, of course.

'Don't suppose you remember who did win?' I said hopefully.

Little Mo was one of those kids who liked lists. He could reel them off just like that. You know the sort of thing – battles in the First World War, famous explorers, bald headed footballers who'd played in the Cup Final.

But not, it seemed, lists of 'Blue Peter' prizewinners.

'Sorry,' he said. 'I only listened for your name.'

It didn't really matter. After all, I'd included a stamped addressed envelope with the false name on it, so I reckoned it was only a question of waiting a day or two for the tickets and that to arrive. Then it'd be straight round to Sharon's and we'd be off to see the sea. Filming was probably on Tuesday so's they could put it out on Wednesday's programme. And that would mean at least one day off school. Better still, our Mam might even have got rid of the Froggy by then. I could hardly wait …

'Oi! Joey! Who was that I seen coming out the house with your Vicki s'morning?'

Beaker Simpson lived a few doors up from us. He was called Beaker on account of he had a big nose which he kept sticking where it wasn't wanted. He was also sweet on our Vicki, which had to mean he was soft in the head. This particular morning, he must have eyeballed our Vicki taking Jean off to school with her, put two and two together and come up with five.

Beaker was like that. Thick.

'It was the fella that runs Dudley Park

Zoo,' I said.

'Huh?'

'Called round and said as how one of their hippos died and wanted to know if our Vicki'd stand in till they could get another one.'

'I'll tell her that, next time I see her,' Beaker growled.

I started off back across the playground.

'Cost you a couple of quid to get in,' I called over my shoulder. 'And don't forget to take her some buns while you're at it.'

'You want to watch yourself with Beaker,' Little Mo said when we got back to class.

I told him not to worry. I knew just how far to push it with Beaker Simpson. He wouldn't pick a fight on me, leastways not while he thought he still had a chance with our Vicki, that is.

First lesson back was supposed to be English, only Miss Shepherd had been away all week and we had this fella instead. Said as how he was a supply teacher or something. Anyway, he supplied us with pens and some paper and said we were to write a story all about monsters from outer space who invaded Earth and took it over.

It sounded a lot like the way the Froggy kid had spread himself all over my room a couple of nights before.

We had to draw a picture, too. I drew one of our Vicki. All green and slimy with lots of arms and legs and the biggest mouth you've ever seen. I took it home with me and stuck it up on the bedroom wall specially where Jean could see it. Bit of luck, it might give him nightmares.

It was that same Friday evening our Mam asked me what I was going to do with Jean over the weekend. Well, that was easy enough. I wasn't doing nothing with Jean over the weekend.

'Anything,' our Mam said sharply.

'What?'

'You said 'nothing' when you meant 'anything',' she corrected me.

Okay, then, so I wasn't doing anything with the kid over the weekend. Meant the same thing, didn't it? And anyway, the Froggy was our Vicki's idea in the first place. Let her look after him.

But our Mam had other ideas.

'You can take Jean to the football with you tomorrow afternoon,' she said.

I had to think fast.

'Give over, Mam, he wouldn't like it,' I

said.

Jean was sitting on the floor, staring at the evening paper. I called over.

'You wouldn't like it, would you, Jean, watching some boring football match all afternoon?'

I stared at him hard and moved my head slowly from side to side, just in case.

He seemed to understand perfectly.

'Oh, no, I should not like to be watching that,' he said frowning.

I breathed a sigh of relief.

'But I am reading the newspaper,' he went on, 'and it is saying the game tomorrow between your Aston Villa and the Arsenal will be a cracker. That is good, I think, yes?'

Depended on your point of view, I suppose. Just then, from where I was sitting, it was bad. Very, very bad.

Why? Well, it's like this.

About a year ago, I got into a spot of bother with the law. Nothing serious, just a bit of fooling round with some mates in town which ended up with me being fished out of an ornamental fountain by some copper who'd dived in under the mistaken impression that I was drowning.

It was pretty embarrassing, I can tell you. But not half as embarrassing as being taken home in a police car with all the neighbours looking out their windows. Our Mam went spare. Specially when the copper told her what I'd been up to. You could see he was narked, too, the way he stood in front of the gas fire with his notebook all wet and soggy and steam coming out his trousers like he was Thomas the Tank Engine.

The upshot of it all was that our Mam said as I wasn't to go up town again on a Saturday. Not unless it was with her or our Vicki.

Can you imagine that? Shopping in town on a Saturday afternoon with your Mam and the original ugly sister? I almost felt like going back and throwing myself in the fountain for good this time.

I didn't, though.

I hit on the idea of going to the football instead.

Not straightaway, of course. Our Mam's not that soft. I left it a couple of weeks and just mooched around the house – making sure I got under her feet, of course, and generally being a right pain in the neck.

It worked a treat.

Then, just to be on the safe side, I got Little Mo to call round one Saturday morning. He was to say how he was going to the football and would I like to come. That was the really clever bit, 'cos our Mam thinks the world of Little Mo. She's always going on about how she wishes I was more like him. Which is pretty unlikely, seeing as his folks come from India and the furthest our Mam's ever been is Walsall to see the illuminations.

'Sorry, Mo,' I said, loud enough so's our Mam could hear. 'I'd love to come to the match with you this afternoon.' I paused. 'But I've promised to help our Mam out round the house and …'

Before you could say 'Up the Villa!' our Mam's suddenly there putting a twenty note in my pocket and pushing the pair of us out the front door.

I split the money fifty-fifty with Little Mo, naturally, and that was it – freedom again.

Not that we ever did go to the football, of course. Little Mo's more your cricketing sort, and as for me, I wouldn't have known the league tables from the multiplication tables. So, it was a case of legging it down to Villa Park to pick up a programme for the match, and then straight into town.

We had it all worked out.

Little Mo'd spend the afternoon going round the museum and art gallery looking at stuffed birds and Egyptian mummies and things. Which left me free to wander round keeping an eye out for fit birds and one Mummy in particular. Then, a quick shuftie through the programme on the way back home and look out for the score on the TV in a shop window, just in case our Mam asked any awkward questions.

Brilliant, eh?

Of course, we could only get away with it every other week or so. Which was another reason why I was miffed about having to look after the Froggy this particular Saturday. It had been two weeks since Villa's last home match and it'd be another two before their next one.

A whole month without going up town!

And all because of some smarmy French kid who knew enough English to suss that a cracker wasn't just something you put cheese on!

Chapter 5

I've got to admit he had me fooled.

All Saturday morning he went on and on about the match and how he'd be able to tell his friends back in Longville all about it. I reckon even our Mam had had enough when one o'clock came and it was time we were going.

'Mohammed not coming with you this week?' she said, seeing us off at the door.

'No,' I said. 'He thinks he's sickening for something.'

What Mo had actually said when I nipped round earlier to tip him off was that the thought of really having to go to the match made him feel sick. So it was near enough the truth.

We didn't say much, Jean and me, on the way to the ground. Come to think of it, we didn't say anything at all. Just walked, sort of side by side but not together, if you know what I mean.

It wasn't long before I sussed a lot of other people must have read the same paper as Jean. The streets round the ground were packed, and every turnstile had a queue a mile long. Looking back now, I suppose it was this that first gave Jean the idea.

We'd just tagged on to the end of a queue marked for 'Juveniles' when he said quietly,

'I am thinking it will be a great disappointment for these fanatics if they do not get in to see the match, Joey.'

He meant the supporters, of course. Though looking round at all those fellas with their scarves and painted faces, I think I preferred his description.

'Yeah,' I said, annoyed that I had to say anything at all.

I edged forward. From where we were standing, the turnstile still seemed a long way off.

'What will we do if we are not getting in to see the match, Joey?'

I had a feeling we weren't likely to see much of it anyway, given the size of some of the so-called 'Juveniles' in the queue ahead of us.

'Dunno,' I said.

I was hoping he'd shut up then, but he didn't. He said,

'Will you also be disappointed, Joey?'

'Yeah,' I said irritably, 'sick as a parrot. Any more questions?'

'I have one more, please, Joey,' he said.

I sighed.

'Go on then,' I said. 'Anything for a bit of peace.'

He stood there looking thoughtful, like he was trying to make up his mind about something.

'Well, go on,' I said, 'what is it?'

'Please, Joey,' he said. 'What is Norm's Caff?'

With so many people around making all that noise, I reckoned I must have heard him wrong.

'Say that again,' I said.

He said it again, slowly this time.

'Please, Joey, what is Norm's Caff?'

I've no idea how long I stood there staring at him. It must have been a while, though, 'cos when I looked round again there was a gap in the queue and some fellas were shouting for us to move up. I shuffled forward. Jean did the same. He was obviously waiting for an answer. I looked at him, puzzled. The kid couldn't have said what I thought he'd said, surely? Maybe he'd been talking French, and it just happened to sound like 'Norm's Caff'. I went to move forward again when the Froggy held out a grubby piece of card towards me. I glanced down at it and frowned. It was one of those cheap address cards, and a pretty tatty one at that. The wording read simply 'NORM'S CAFF – BIRMINGHAM' with a telephone number underneath.

'Where'd you get that from?' I said.

'You are not knowing this Norm's Caff, Joey?' He sounded disappointed.

Oh, I knew it all right. What I couldn't fathom was how a kid who'd never even been to England before, let alone Birmingham, had got to hear of it. And what was he doing with a tatty address card for the place? I mean, it wasn't exactly Buckingham Palace or the Houses of Parliament he was asking about. They're special places, the sort you'd expect even most Froggy kids to have heard of. But you could hardly describe Norm's Caff as the sort of place you'd find coming up in a lesson on famous English landmarks.

The queue moved forward again. Another five minutes and we'd be inside the ground. It dawned on me I still hadn't answered his question.

'Yeah, 'course I know Norm's,' I said. 'It's a tranny – a transport café, down near the motorway. Why?'

He caught hold my arm.

'You will take me there, Joey, this Norm's Caff. Please. It is important.'

Now, I don't mind the likes of Sharon holding my hand sometimes if there's no-one else around and if it makes her feel good. But no way was I walking into a crowd of 40,000 footy fans in broad daylight arm-in-arm with some Froggy kid – even if he did have a girl's name!

'Gerroff,' I said, pushing his hand away. 'And anyway, why the big deal about some tranny caff all of a sudden? I thought you wanted to see the football.'

'It is very important to me, Joey. The honour of my family is at stake here. A matter of life and death, as you English say.'

Well, I'd heard of taking the game seriously, but this was ridiculous. I didn't suss he meant the caff until he starts getting all worked up, and he's there pulling at my arm again and trying to drag me out of the queue.

'Please, Joey. You take me there now. We go there now, Joey. Please!'

'Give over, will yer!' I shouted. 'You'll lose us our places.'

For someone dead keen to see a football match, he was certainly going a funny way about it. One of the nick-nick brigade must have thought so too, judging by the way he was eyeballing the pair of us. I remembered seeing that sort of ''Ello, 'ello, what's going on 'ere' look on a copper's face once before. It was just after I'd been fished out of the ornamental fountain that time. It spelt trouble, which was what we'd be in if I couldn't get the Froggy to calm down and stop doing his one-man impression of a crowd of football hooligans.

I glanced over his shoulder. Any second now and the long arm of the law would reach out and we'd both be nabbed. I could just imagine how that would go down with our Mam, not to mention Mrs Lewis.

I read somewhere that a drowning man sees his whole life pass in front of his eyes just before he goes under for the third time. With me, it was the thought of years of Saturday afternoons spent traipsing round the shops after our Mam and Vicki that finally did it.

'Okay, okay,' I hissed. 'We'll go – now – this minute. Only let go me arm, will yer. You'll get us arrested or summat!'

To this day, I'm still not sure whether Jean planned it, or whether it was just one of those things that sort of happen.

There we are, middle of Saturday afternoon, outside the footy ground, surrounded by people and about to be arrested – and what does he do? Only goes and kisses me, doesn't he?"

No kidding. Puts his hands on my shoulders and kisses me. Twice. Once on each cheek.

If you think I was shocked, you should have seen the copper. Stopped dead in his tracks he did, like he'd suddenly walked into a plate-glass door that he didn't know was there.

It was now or never.

'Come on!' I yelled, and hared off down the road. I was praying the Froggy had enough sense to do the same.

He did. He passed me half way down the hill.

He was waiting for me when I turned the corner into Park Street, and grinning from ear to ear.

'What's so funny?' I panted. I was still narked about him kissing me in front of all those people.

He laughed.

'It is a good story, yes?' he said. 'I am in England only a few days and already I am, as you say, on the run from your policemen.'

Chapter 6

It took us about twenty minutes to reach Norm's Caff. I made a point of walking slowly – mainly 'cos I needed to get my breath back after the previous little episode. And I wanted time to think over a few things. Like what I was going to tell our Mam about the match, and what exactly I was doing going to Norm's Caff on a Saturday afternoon, and what was so important about a crummy tranny caff anyway.

And like why did I have a feeling deep down somewhere that this Jean character never had the slightest intention of going to the match in the first place.

A matter of life and death he'd called it. Looking at the single storey concrete block with its corrugated iron roof and bars on the windows, I could well believe it. The death part, anyway. Only you sort of got the impression we were about ten years too late for the funeral.

'Not exactly the Taj Mahal, is it?' I said.

The Froggy didn't answer. He was already halfway across the road. I caught up with him on the car park, a piece of waste ground that looked like something you wouldn't drive a moon buggy over. Except for an articulated lorry parked over the far side, the place was deserted.

Jean was standing in front of a sign that read   V   NI HT   P   G.

I explained it meant OVERNIGHT PARKING. Leastways it had until someone called Roger King nicked all the letters of his name off of it. Jean nodded and started towards the caff door.

That did it as far as I was concerned. A joke was a joke, but, like me, this particular one had gone far enough. I wanted some answers.

'Inside,' he said. 'I will tell you inside.'

'In there?' I said. 'No way. Listen, from what I've heard there's fellas gone in there and never been seen again. Me, I like living – so anything you've got to say, you say it out here. Right? Then I'll tell you whether I'm coming in or not.'

It was a lie of course, There was nothing the Froggy could possibly say that would get me inside Norm's Caff, not even in broad daylight.

He must have guessed as much. One minute he's standing there listening to me rabbitting on. The next, he's through the door quick as you like.

It fair shook me that did, I can tell you. Either he was a whole lot braver than I'd given him credit for, or else just plain bananas.

I settled for him being bananas – in which case they'd skin him alive.
I decided to wait. Chances were he'd be back out even quicker than he went in. And the least I could do would be to call an ambulance.

I stared out across the car park. It was shot full of lumps and bumps and holes, and I got to thinking what our Mam'd do to me when I told her. I never did like the sight of blood, specially my own. Then there was that teacher-woman, Mrs Lewis. She'd have to be told, of course. Though I didn't suppose she'd thank me much for solving her problem of how to get twenty-one Froggy kids back to France when there should've only been twenty in the first place. And as for the expenses she'd promised our Mam for looking after him …

Thinking of Mrs Lewis got me wondering again. I mean, she didn't look the sort to make mistakes. So if she'd booked for twenty kids to come over, and twenty-one had arrived, how come no-one had sussed this extra pair of Frogs-legs hopping round the place? Like on the ferry, for instance.

So then, how had he managed it? I mean, he could hardly have been mistaken for one of the crew, now could he? So how come no-one had asked to see his ticket – always assuming he had one, of course. And what about getting through Customs and that? Then there were the other kids, the ones Mrs Lewis had been expecting. Surely they must have noticed him. So why hadn't they said something? And why …

''Ere, your name Joey?'

Jump? I must have leapt a foot in the air.

I looked round and there's this enormous great fella with a beard and tattoos all down his arms coming towards me from the direction of the caff. I suppose I must have nodded, given that the rest of me was shaking like a jelly anyway.

Man-mountain jerked a thumb over one massive shoulder.

'Yer wanted. Inside.'

I wanted to run but my legs just stayed put.

He came closer. I could see he was grinning.

'Wh … What for?' I stammered.

I could read the words LOVE and

HATE tattooed across the knuckles of his fists. He came up level with me, blocking out the sunlight. I shut my eyes.

"Cos yer mate in there says to tell yer yer tea's goin' cold. See yer!'

When I opened my eyes again, he was gone. I turned round. He was all of twenty metres away and unlocking the cab of the artic before I got my voice back.

'Thanks for nothing, mate,' I whispered under my breath. And then louder this time, 'Have a good trip!'

He waved and climbed into the cab. Seconds later the diesel engine roared into life, spewing clouds of fumes from the exhaust. I stood watching as the huge truck bumped and rattled its way out onto the main road heading south towards the motorway.

I turned round. So, my tea was getting cold, was it? Well, we'd soon see about that. Fists clenched, I strode back towards the caff. This was something that couldn't wait. And I didn't care whether he went bleating to our Mam or to Mrs Lewis. He was going to get it and get it real good after what I'd just been through because of him.

But first I was going to get some answers.

I pushed open the door and peered in

– making sure I kept a hold of the handle, just in case like.

The first thing that hit me was the smell. It was awful. Sort of greasy bacon and smoke and sweaty socks all rolled into one. The floor was bare grey concrete, paint was peeling off the walls, and the whole place had a damp, musty feel to it. And it was dark. A layer of dirt and grime coated the windows. What light there was came from a couple of fluorescent strip-lights dangling precariously from the ceiling. I suppose the idea was so that you couldn't see what it was you were eating. Though why anyone in their right mind should want to eat in a place like that was beyond me.

Whoever Norm was, he certainly didn't go out of his way to attract custom. Which probably explained why, except for a wino slumped over the table nearest the door, Jean had the caff all to himself. He was sitting on the far side of the room, swigging a can of Coke, and looking for all the world like he owned the place. There was mug of something on the table in front of him. My tea going cold, no doubt.

I stepped inside and shut the door behind me. The wino stirred, shifted position slightly, and went back to sleep again. I made my way between the empty tables. Jean looked up and grinned. I scowled back and pulled up one of the cheap plastic chairs. It scraped noisily on the concrete floor. Jean pushed the mug of tea across the table towards me. The mug was chipped in several places and there were brown stains round the rim. I left it where it was. I gave Jean a look which said I wasn't his mate and even if I was it would take more than a smile and a mug of cold tea to get round me this time – a lot more.

So, if he wanted me to stay, he'd better start making with the right noises.

He nodded, and I sat down.

Chapter 7

I don't usually hang about for long when kids start going on about their dads. Not that I'm sore or anything about mine skipping off before I had a chance to get to know him. It's just that I haven't really got anything to say when the subject does come up. Which round here isn't very often anyway, on account of there's almost as many kids without dads as with them.

It's different with mams, of course. Specially with mine and our Vicki's.

Couple of years ago, I had to write this essay in school. 'Man or Woman of the Year' the teacher called it. You had to pick someone and say what they'd done to make them special. I did all about our Mam, and I remember being dead narked when this teacher put '6/10 Could do better'. Underneath I wrote that our Mam did the best she could, and I reckon the teacher knew what I was getting at, 'cos he didn't say any more about it.

Jean's old man was called Maurice – Maurice Boniface. He was forty-one, the boss of a big company, and he was in a lot of trouble. Leastways, that's how Jean saw it. I say that, 'cos as far as Jean knew, his old man wasn't aware of any trouble. There'd been a problem and Mr Boniface thought he'd solved it. Jean reckoned differently.

And listening to him explaining it, I did get to thinking that maybe, just this once, Jean was right.

Maurice Boniface owned a fleet of trucks. Couple of dozen of them, Jean said. They drove all over Europe, helping people move house when they were leaving one country to go and live in another. Which made Jean's old fella a sort of international 'Mr Shifter', if you see what I mean. Jean said as how there were always people wanting to move, and that a couple of trucks made regular trips between France and England using the ferries or the tunnel, whichever was most convenient.

Nice work if you can get it, I thought. So what was the problem? And why all the mystery? Most of all, what did it have to do with us being in Norm's Caff on a Saturday afternoon?

Jean leant across the table.

'Some months ago,' he said, almost in a whisper, 'two men are coming to see my father in his office. They say they would like certain things brought from England in his lorries. But they do not say what things exactly. They are offering him money, naturally, but my father does not like these men. He has, as you say, a nose for trouble – and these men are smelling.'

'They weren't locals, then? You know, fellas he'd seen before?'

Jean shook his head.

'No. One was British. The other was, I regret to say, a Frenchman.'

'So your old man said no and they turned nasty and beat him up, eh?'

I was hoping to get to the interesting bit in rather less time than it was taking him. Besides, the sooner we were out in the fresh air again, the better I'd like it.

In fact, Mr Boniface's visitors hadn't turned nasty. Rather, they'd gone away and come back a few days later with an improved offer. The upshot of it was, Jean's old man told them where to get off, and that was the last he'd seen of them. End of problem, at least as far as he was concerned.

And how come Jean knew all this? It seemed Mr Boniface had told Mrs Boniface, and Jean had overheard them talking one night when he was supposed to be upstairs asleep.

I knew the sort of thing he meant.

There's times I creep out on the landing and listen in if I think our Mam's telling Vicki summat she doesn't want me hearing.

But that apart, I have to admit I was disappointed. At the very least I expected stories of illegal immigrants or trucks being hijacked and blown up and high-speed chases and drivers being forced off the road. You know the sort of thing. All he'd told me so far was a big fat zero.

Jean must have sussed what I was thinking.

'Please be patient with me, Joey,' he said. 'I am telling you it all from the beginning so that you will understand and perhaps help me.'

'Yeah, well, we'll have to see about that,' I said. Meaning you didn't catch Joey Edwards that easily. I'd want to know a lot more before I suddenly started playing the Good Samaritan. Like, what was in it for me, for example.

'As I was saying,' he went on, 'my father does not see these men again. He is pleased then, and does not talk of them since. But me, I am seeing them in the town several times. They do not know me but I am knowing them from how my father describes them. Always they are talking with the same driver, a man who is working for my father. His name is Michel.'

I stopped myself laughing just in time. I mean, whoever heard of a truck driver called Michel? It was like calling a ballet dancer Fred or Alf or something.

The point was, of course, that Jean had sussed this Michel fella was up to no good. Well, he would be, wouldn't he, with a name like that. So anyway, Jean starts keeping an eye on this Michel. Two eyes actually, and a pair of ears, and a nose, on account of he was smelling a rat, as he put it. Oh yeah, and he also kept a diary. Leastways, that's what he called the scrap of paper he handed me to look at. He might as well have given me a Chinese recipe for all the sense I could make of it. First off, there was the handwriting, which looked like a one-legged spider with gout had done it. Secondly, it was all in French.

I was just about to own up when suddenly I heard voices and the door to the caff was flung open. Jean glanced up sharply. Me, I nearly leapt out of my skin. I turned round so fast, my knee caught the table-leg and I ended up slopping cold tea all over Jean's bit of paper. It was so obvious, even the wino stirred himself long enough to suss what all the racket was about. There was even a moment when I thought he was going to say something, but he obviously thought better of it and shut his mouth again.

As for me, I was just wishing the ground would open up and swallow me. Specially when I saw how one of the newcomers was fixed. Six feet high, three feet wide, and all solid muscle, even where his brain should have been. A proper Guy the Gorilla if ever I saw one. He didn't look the sort who could walk and chew gum at the same time, though I didn't suppose anyone ever bothered telling him that to his face – leastways not more than once.

And as for his mate – talk about fat! You know those 'before' and 'after' pictures of people who've been on a diet? Well, he was most definitely the 'before' one. I reckoned you could boil an egg in the time it'd take to walk all the way round him. Come to think of it, he looked a bit like an egg himself – bald on top and fat in the middle. He also had this funny way of breathing. Sort of loud and heavy like he'd been running after a bus and missed it. 'Cept in his condition, I couldn't imagine him running after anything. He only just about made it to a table down the other end near the counter.

I know you shouldn't stare but I couldn't help it. Specially when, right on cue, Norm appeared from behind one of those shredded plastic curtains that are supposed to keep flies out of the kitchen. Though if Norm himself was anything to go by, I couldn't imagine any self-respecting fly wanting to go near the place. He looked like I imagined one of his bacon sarnies would be – sort of white and limp and greasy. He hadn't shaved, and he had on one of those white coats that you see waiters and hospital doctors wearing. 'Cept that his wasn't white – more a sort of dirty grey colour with tea and coffee stains all over it.

I sussed that Heavy Breather and the Gorilla were regulars the way Norm served up two mugs of something without waiting for them to order. Heavy Breather was carrying a newspaper which he opened and spread out on the table and all three of them sat there looking at it. Proper little readers' corner it was, too. I just hoped there were lots of pictures in it for the Gorilla's sake.

Not that I was having much more success with what Jean had given me to look at. Specially now the paper was all limp and soggy where I'd slopped tea over it. I did suss it was probably some sort of timetable on account of there were lots of numbers and the odd word here and there such as 'Birmingham' and 'London'.

I gave it him back.

'Beats me,' I said, trying to make it sound like I didn't much care anyway – which, to be honest, I didn't.

He explained then, about the diary and that. Said as how it was a copy he'd made of this Michel character's work schedule. You know the sort of thing – times, dates, distance covered and so on. He'd done it by sneaking a look at the computer in his old man's office now and again. So that was where he'd got the address card from – the one with 'Norm's Caff' printed on it?

Jean shook his head.

'No,' he said. 'That is by chance. When the lorries are parked some evenings, I am earning money for the pocket by cleaning out their insides. One day I find this card. It is in Michel's cab, of course.'

'Yeah, well, it would be, wouldn't it?' I said.

He grinned.

'Michel is there and I ask him what is this Norm's Caff. I mean to joke, but he is angry then and tells me to be minding my own business. He is trying to take the card from me but I run and hide. After, he does not mention the card again, but he is angry still and does not want me to clean the cab.'

'Well, go on then,' I said. 'Let's have another eyeball at it. Maybe we missed summat.'

There wasn't much to miss. Just the three words, 'NORM'S CAFF – BIRMINGHAM' and a telephone number. I turned it over. Nothing. So how come all the aggro on Michel's part?

Jean shrugged.

'There is more,' he said.

I was all ears.

'Last week' – Jean pointed to the actual date on the scrap of paper – 'I overhear Michel talking on the telephone in the office.'

That was more like it, I thought. A bit of cloak and dagger stuff at last.

'I am late with my cleaning,' Jean explained, 'and for everyone else the day has finished. I am returning the key of the lorry when I hear Michel's voice. I listen, of course, but it is not easy. The door is closed and he speaks quietly. He talks to someone who is called, I think, Mac. 'Big Mac', he keeps saying. 'Oui, Big Mac' and 'Non, Big Mac'. This is a British name, Joey – this 'Big Mac'?'

Well, unless the fella was ordering a burger and fries, it had to be, didn't it?

'And he is laughing,' Jean went on. 'I do not like the sound. It is evil,' and here his eyes narrowed. 'I am thinking perhaps he laughs at my father.'

I could see he was getting upset by then, so I didn't say anything. I just sat there, shuffling my feet round and generally feeling sort of awkward. Which is how come I started taking an interest in what was happening at the table near the counter.

The three members of the readers' circle had obviously found what they were looking for in the paper. They were all smiles as Norm read something aloud which Heavy Breather wrote in a notebook. Even the Gorilla was making contented grunting noises rocking backwards and forwards in his chair.

Suddenly, I was real curious to know what three fellas like them found so interesting in a newsie that they had to copy it down. You could bet your life it wasn't the recipe-of-the-day. But, short of going over and asking them, I didn't suppose there was much chance of finding out. Unless …

'Look, Jean,' I said, 'we'd better be off. You can tell me the rest of it on the way into town. We'll get a bus from there. And you'd better start thinking what you want to tell our Mam about the match, okay?'

He nodded and stood up, scraping his chair on the floor.

'I'll do that,' I said, picking up the half-empty mug of tea.

I started making my way between the tables. Norm didn't look up from the paper, but I saw the cigarette twitch in the corner of his mouth when I put the mug down on the counter. I was going to say something about smoking in a public place but thought better of it.

'Ta, Norm,' I said, sort of casual like.

He grunted and dropped cigarette ash on the paper.

I stood there, staring down at the table. It was the Gorilla who cottoned on first.

'Seen enough, kid?'

I took a chance and put on my best butter-wouldn't-melt look. If it didn't work, I could end up spread all over the floor and looking like one of Norm's sarnies.

'Anything in the paper 'bout the footy, mister?' I said loudly enough so's they wouldn't hear my knees knocking together.

'Huh?' growled the Gorilla.

I did a quick mental translation.

'Villa and Arsenal. Me and me mate

couldn't get in.'

Norm glanced up from the paper.

'Too early, kid,' he said irritably. 'They'll still be playing.'

'Oh, yeah,' I said, trying to sound disappointed.

I was an' all. The newsie was open at the page where they have announcements and things and those free adverts where people sell stuff they don't want. So, after all that, it seemed they were really only on the look-out for a second-hand Encyclopedia Brittanica for the Gorilla or maybe an exercise bike for Heavy Breather.

'Hold on, son.' It was Heavy Breather. I froze. 'I'll look on the net for you,' he said, picking up his phone and flicking through the screens with a podgy finger. 'If there's been an early goal it'll probably say.'

He had a strange voice. The sort you'd expect a rattlesnake to have if it could speak – croaky and rasping, like he had a piece of sandpaper wedged in his throat. Scared me more than the Gorilla did, that voice.

He held the phone up so's I could see the screen.

I said, 'Ta anyway,' and let them get back to the newsie.

Jean was standing by the door. He

followed me outside.

'Those men,' he said. 'You did not say you knew them.'

It was his turn to look puzzled. I was going to enjoy this. I stood there squinting and taking in dollops of fresh air.

'Those two? Oh, yeah,' I lied, 'friends of mine. Go back a long way, we do.'

Why not, I thought. I still owed him one, after all.

'And what are they saying to you, these 'friends' of yours, Joey?'

'Showed me something, didn't they? About what we were saying earlier.' I paused. 'Seems you got it wrong, Jean.'

He looked shocked. I waited a few seconds longer.

'About the match being a cracker. Load of rubbish apparently. Nil nil at half-time.'

I grinned and started off across the car park.

Chapter 8

That night, we went over the whole business from start to finish – or rather Jean did. He filled in some of the details, too. Like how he'd made up his mind to come to England with the idea of finding out what exactly this Michel fella was up to.

Trouble was, that's all he did have – an idea.

Michel, he knew, was due in England sometime in the next few days. He was supposed to be picking up a lorry-load of stuff for a couple of wrinklies who were retiring to live in France. Jean's idea, such as it was, involved following Michel round the place and generally trying to keep an eye out for any funny business.

And that was about as far as he'd got. The fact that he didn't know exactly where in England this Michel would be at any one time didn't seem to bother him. And when I asked how he intended keeping tabs on a lorry that could be bombing round the country at fifty miles an hour, he just shrugged and said,

'There are ways, perhaps ...'

So I changed the subject then. I asked him about the journey and that instead and how come no-one had sussed him.

'It is the half-term holiday in my school,' he said. 'Some children are coming to stay in England. I am not one of these, but I still come.'

We were talking with the lights out on account of we were supposed to be asleep. I heard him laugh quietly.

'Children without their teachers. It is fun, is it not? They run and chase and make noise. People do not check. They are not wishing to keep them longer than is necessary.'

'Yeah,' I said, 'but what about on the ferry?'

'It is not full. There are seats. I buy my own ticket. I have my passport – and children are always going to the toilet. For the rest ...'

I heard his fingers click in the dark.

I had to hand it to him – he was a cool one all right. But wouldn't his folks be worried? I mean, it stood to reason they'd notice when he suddenly wasn't around the place.

He went quiet for a bit. Our mam had fixed him up with a spare mattress on the floor and I could hear his breathing coming from the other side of the room.

'I tell them I am with friends,' he said eventually. 'We are in tents in the country away from the town.'

'Camping, you mean?'

'Yes,' he said. 'It is not unusual. I am in tents many times before. But now it is a lie. I do not like saying lies to my parents.'

Odd, that. All the things he had said and done, and yet it was the bit about conning his folks that got to him most.

Oh, and the big match? Nil nil, apparently. So we hadn't missed much after all!

Jean was out most of Sunday. Poor kid, he never stood a chance. Had it all worked out she did, our Vicki. Arrived downstairs about ten o'clock, all dolled up like a dog's dinner and with them heels that make her look like the Leaning Tower of Pisa when she walks.

Jean's eyes nearly popped out of his head. And no wonder. You've heard the one about Helen of Troy's face launching a thousand ships? I tell you, one look at our Vicki's and there's not a sailor who wouldn't have jumped overboard and drowned himself there and then.

Jean wasn't going to get away so easily. Our Vicki saw to that. Said as how she wanted to show him the sights of

Birmingham. I said as how that shouldn't take more than ten minutes, and had she included herself on the list. As it was, it took them the whole day and most of the evening, too, so that I was already in bed by the time they got back.

To be honest, I didn't mind in the least.

Their going walkies meant I had most of the day to think over what he'd said. Not that it got me very far, though. What I had, it seemed, was a load of questions and no answers. Take this business with the lorry, for example. I mean, what could anybody possibly want stashed away in the back of a furniture van going from England to France? Drugs? Guns?

All right, so I know you read about that sort of thing happening, or maybe see it on telly or at the films. But be honest. Whoever heard of a movie called 'The Brum Connection' or 'The Solihull Job'? And how many kids do you know who've actually seen things like that going on or been involved in them? See what I mean? So why should it be any different for me or Jean?

Okay, so we all do things we shouldn't, like nicking the odd choccy bar or wagging school now and again. But it's all mostly kids' stuff. And the worst you can expect is probably a clip round the earhole if yer Mam finds out.

'Course, you always get one or two who never really grow out of it. Then, instead of choccy bars, it's shops and cars and other people's houses, and so on, until eventually they get caught. In which case, it's back to the bars again for them – the sort you look out through from places like Dartmoor and Wormwood Scrubs.

No, the way I saw it was like this. If Jean was right and this Michel character was up to no good, then it was almost certainly premier league stuff. In which case, count me out. And the same ought to go for Jean if he had any sense.

I decided to put off telling him till morning. After a whole day spent with our Vicki, the least the kid deserved was a good night's sleep. Besides, I wanted to be up early myself, ready for the big moment when my tickets arrived in the post from 'Blue Peter'.

Chapter 9

Monday was a disaster.

I suppose I should have been prepared for the worst when the fella on breakfast telly read out my horoscope for the day. 'Horrorscope' would have been more accurate, I reckon.

'Life today will be full of little disappointments,' he said – and that was the good news. 'Events will tend to move more rapidly than you would like, causing you no end of problems. You can expect to run into trouble with a figure of authority. Not a favourable aspect where affairs of the heart are concerned or for those of you contemplating a journey. You may suffer from periodic bouts of depression.'

He was right an' all. In fact, I got pretty depressed just listening to him.

I reckoned the post would cheer me up, though.

There wasn't any.

I was looking out specially, and couldn't believe it when Postman Patel went legging straight past the front door in his vest and underpants. First off, I reckoned as he'd been attacked again by the two big Alsatians from number eleven. Then I remembered. He was supposed to be in training for the London marathon and this was his way of keeping fit.

Well, I'd heard of post-haste but this was ridiculous.

I caught up with him at the corner of Bankdale Street just as he was coming to the end of his round. Trouble was, by then I was so out of breath I could hardly speak. I just sort of stumbled along beside him making funny gasping noises and pointing to the bag on his shoulder.

Postman Patel obviously wasn't into charades.

'Well, well,' he said, grinning down at me, 'if it isn't young Joey from number twenty-six. This is a surprise.'

It was an' all. I hadn't realised keeping fit made you feel quite so ill. It got worse. Postman Patel's bag was empty – leastways, there was absolutely nothing there for anyone at number twenty-six.

'Race you back to the sorting-office if you like, Joey,' said Postman Patel, hoisting the limp bag over his shoulder.

He didn't wait for an answer. Not that I could have given one anyway on account of there was this sort of red mist in front of my eyes and I felt like I was dying. Instead, he put on what I think the commentators call a spurt down the back straight and disappeared round the next corner. I don't suppose they've got a phrase for what I did. 'Joey Edwards, knackered, crawled in through the front door' hasn't got quite the same ring to it, if you see what I mean.

I was lying on the sofa, wondering how I was going to tell Sharon the trip was off, when our Vicki came in. I sort of got the impression she was disappointed to see me.

'Oh, it's you,' she said. 'You're up early, our Joey.'

'Yeah,' I said. 'Been trying to catch up on my mail, haven't I?'

She pulled one of her faces, but it wasn't much of an improvement.

'They teach you to write, then, at that school of yours.'

'Yeah,' I said, 'and count.' I held up two fingers. 'See.'

For once she didn't get mad and go running off to tell our Mam.

'Where's Jean?' she asked.

'Dunno. Still in bed, I suppose. Why?'

'Nothing,' she said, meaning that there was something. 'It's just that I thought he might want to see me off.'

'Told you before,' I said. 'You shouldn't think. You're not equipped for it. Anyway, what's all this about seeing you off? I thought he was coming to school with you.'

'Can't today,' she said. 'I've got a Geography field-trip and Jean can't come 'cos it's part of an exam so our Mam says he's to go to school with you instead. So there!'

'With me!' I sat bolt upright and then wished I hadn't. My legs felt like they'd never walk again. Luckily my brain was still working. 'But he can't,' I said quickly. 'I'm having a day off. I've … I've gorra pain in me leg. In both legs!'

'You'll have one in the back of yer 'ead an' all if you don't get off that sofa and ready for school,' said our Mam. 'Breakfast's on the table. Move!'

I tell you, when our Mam's prowling round the house in her slippers, she's more deadly than a nuclear submarine. Carries more clout, too. Which is why I didn't hang about, 'cept to stick my tongue out at our Vicki who must have seen her come in through the kitchen door.

To cap it all, the cornflakes had gone soggy and I even had to put up with our Vicki sitting opposite me all through breakfast. I felt like a condemned man eating his last meal before the execution. 'Cept I'd have liked the blindfold there and then. It would've made life difficult finding my mouth with the spoon, but at least I'd have been spared the sight of my sister's ugly mug grinning from ear to ear.

Chapter 10

I didn't let on to Jean that I was choked about being lumbered with him again. I mean, it was hardly his fault if our Vicki had to spend the day making daisy-chains and collecting cow-pats or whatever it is they do on Geography field-trips. And I don't mind admitting the kid had gone up a bit in my estimation after that business in Norm's Caff.

No, I was thinking more of what the other kids would say when they saw him. Like Beaker Simpson, for instance.

'Just leave the talking to me, right?' I said. We were making our way through a gap in the wall where the school gate used to be. 'Anybody speaks to you, ignore them. Ten to one the teachers won't even notice you anyway.'

Sure enough, Beaker and a couple of his mates were waiting outside the classroom.

'Remember what I told you,' I hissed as we walked along the corridor. 'Just act dumb and you'll be alright. I know how to handle this lot.'

'Well, well,' said Beaker as we came up level with him. 'What have we here, lads? Little joey Edwards bringing his pet frog to school by the look of it. Not allowed that isn't, Joey.' He patted me on the head. 'School rules – no pets in the classroom. Specially frogs. Ain't that right, lads?'

His two goons grunted. I went to push past them. Beaker caught hold of my arm.

'What's the big hurry, Joey? Registration's not for another ten minutes yet. How's about we have a closer look at this here pet of yours, eh?'

'Leave off, Beaker,' I said. 'The kid's alright. Besides, he doesn't speak much English.'

Beaker's mood suddenly turned nasty.

'Oh yeah? Well I heard different. Or didn't you know about frog-legs here and your Vicki?'

'Cobblers!' I said. 'He's not interested in our Vicki. It's her that's …'

I stopped myself just in time. Beaker eyed me suspiciously. He scowled and pointed an accusing finger at Jean.

'So how come he spends all Sunday chatting her up, eh?'

So that was it. I should have guessed. There wasn't much happened round our way that Beaker didn't get to hear of – specially if it concerned our Vicki.

'Who did, the Froggy?' I said, trying to

sound surprised.

'Got it in one, kid,' Beaker snarled. He pushed his face real close to mine so's all I could see was his nose twitching. 'Proper little Romeo, ain't he?'

I didn't mean to laugh. It was just that I'd never thought of our Vicki as a Juliet before.

I stopped laughing when I found I couldn't breathe on account of Beaker had his hands round my throat, and there was this gap between my feet and where the floor should have been. He never did have much of a sense of humour.

I had to think fast. I was Beaker Simpson's mate remember. Imagine what he'd do to someone he didn't like – Jean, for instance. It might be one way of solving Mrs Lewis's little problem for her, but I couldn't see it doing much for Anglo-French relations. There was also the question of the money our Mam was supposed to get for looking after him.

'Okay,' I croaked, 'so what if the kid was with our Vicki? That's the idea innit? She's supposed to show him round the place and help him with his English lessons, see.'

'So what'd he kiss her for, then?' growled Beaker, letting me drop with a thud.

It was like asking why rats eat poison. I couldn't believe it. I mean, who in their right mind could possibly want to kiss our Vicki? Not Jean, surely? She must have tricked him into it. But why? I mean, he was hardly her sort. He was, well, good-looking and intelligent for starters.

'I ain't kissed nobody who's bin learning me English,' Beaker went on. 'How's about you, Joey? You go round kissing people who learn you, huh?'

'Course not,' I said. 'And that goes for Jean, too, don't it, Jean?'

He frowned and looked puzzled.

'Je ne comprends pas, Joey,' he said.

I took a chance.

'There you are, Beaker,' I said triumphantly, 'what did I tell you? The kid never went near our Vicki.'

'He's lying,' Beaker snarled. 'I saw 'em. Last night. Coming down the road they was. Holding hands. An' just before they went into your house they stopped an' I saw 'im kiss her.'

His fists bunched as he glared angrily across at Jean.

'Sure it weren't the other way round, Beaker?' I said quickly. 'You know, her kissing him like?'

He stared at me blankly. I reckoned it was time Beaker Simpson and me did some straight talking, man to man sort of thing. I put my hand on his arm.

'Just between ourselves, Beaker,' I said, lowering my voice, 'I reckon it was all our Vicki's doing. She was hoping you'd see her with the Froggy just so's you'd get jealous. Girls are like that, you know – specially our Vicki. Question is, of course, whether you're going to let her get away with it. Know what I mean?'

Clever stuff, eh? Talk about killing two birds with one stone. This way I could get me and Jean off the hook and land our Vicki in it at the same time. Things were looking up. Specially with Beaker nodding his head the way people do when they haven't a clue what you're on about but don't want you to think they're stupid.

I didn't think Beaker Simpson was stupid – I knew he was.

'What d'ye reckon I should do, then, Joey?' Beaker grunted.

'About our Vicki? Nothing – leastways not yet,' I said. 'Play her at her own game. Pretend you've lost interest. Make a point of knocking around with someone else for a while. Best of all, spread the word as how you think she's just a dumb blonde bimbo who's not worth bothering about, you know the sort of thing. Come to think of it, I wouldn't mind helping you out a bit as far as that's concerned.'

'Thanks, Joey, you're a mate,' Beaker said.

I wished he could have made it sound more convincing.

'Well, that's what mates are for, ain't it?' I said. 'Stick together, show them who's boss and that, eh?'

He nodded glumly.

'Dumb - blonde - bimbo,' he said slowly.

'That's the idea,' I said. 'And cheer up. Few days of that should do the trick. You'll have her eating out the palm of your hand in no time.'

You see pigeons doing that sort of thing, don't you? Eating out of people's hands. Horrible things, pigeons. All beak and bum – just like our Vicki.

So far, so good. Now all I had to do was smooth things over between Jean and Beaker Simpson.

'Over here, Jean,' I said. 'There's someone I want you to meet.'

He took a couple of steps forward.

'Je ne comprends ...' he began.

'It's okay,' I said, shutting him up quickly. Beaker wasn't that stupid. 'We heard you the first time. And anyway, you can speak English from here on in. You know, like our Vicki's been teaching you.'

'But Joey,' he said, 'you are telling me ...'

'Forget it,' I said. 'This here's Beaker Simpson. Beaker's a mate of mine. Ain't that right, Beaker?'

Beaker nodded, leastways I think he did.

'I am hearing of this Beaky Simpleton,' Jean said, none too friendly like.

'Yeah, well, you would've, wouldn't you?' I said, dropping the hint and wishing he'd take a bit more care with other people's names. 'Beaker's a friend of our Vicki's. A special friend.'

It should have been as plain as the nose on Beaker's face what I was getting at.

'This I am hearing also,' Jean said coldly.

Any other time and I'd have asked him how his mate Noddy was getting along. I gave it a miss on account of I didn't like the way him and Beaker were eyeballing each other.

'Anyway,' I said, 'I just thought as you'd like to meet Beaker and say hello and that way we can all be mates.'

Jean looked at me sort of funny like.

'Well, what are you waiting for?' I said. 'Say 'Hello, Beaker'.'

''Ello, Beaky,' Jean said.

Beaker grunted something that I translated for Jean as being 'Hello, Jean'.

Jean didn't look convinced.

'I am thinking this Beaky is not my friend,' he said suddenly.

'Rubbish!' I said. 'He's over the moon about it, aren't you, Beaky – I mean Beaker?'

'Yeah. Over the moon,' Beaker growled.

'No, you are not understanding, Joey,' Jean said. 'I am not wanting this friendship. There is a problem you see, with Beaky and myself – and the lovely Victoria.'

Now, whatever problems Beaker did have, earwigging wasn't one of them – specially not where our Vicki's name was concerned.

'Dumb blonde bimbo,' he muttered.

Jean looked up, startled.

'Mon dieu!' he exclaimed. 'Such language I am hearing! And of the lovely Victoria!'

'Dumb – blonde – stupid - bimbo,' said Beaker, right on cue. He was obviously getting the hang of it, and not before time, too.

They say pride goes before a fall. There I was, just congratulating myself on a job well done, when – Smack! Jean up and lands Beaker Simpson one right across the face!

'That,' said Jean, 'is for the honour of the lovely Victoria. And this,' – he caught Beaker smack on the other cheek – 'this I do for my friend Joey.'

With friends like that, who needed enemies?

I was stunned. Not half as stunned as Beaker Simpson was, of course. But then, I wasn't the one standing there with two red cheeks and a red nose. He looked like something out of a Punch and Judy show. And there was no mistaking which particular Judy he was going to punch first.

Someone shouted 'Run, Jean!' and I must have been halfway down the corridor before I realised it was me doing the shouting! I reckon I had a metre start – which meant I ran slap-bang into Mr Butcher exactly one second before the rest of them did.

Butch – Mr Butcher – was the Deputy

Head. And he didn't mince words.

'Up against the wall!' he yelled. 'All of you!'

I went and stood between Jean and Beaker Simpson. Talk about being the meat in a sandwich!

'Names?' said Mr Butcher, fishing out the little black book he kept specially for the purpose. 'As if I couldn't guess.'

He stopped writing when he came to Jean.

'Bonny Face … Bonny Face … I don't recall hearing that name before. Whose form are you in, Face?'

'New boy, sir, starting this morning,' I said quickly. At least it saved the bother of explaining.

'Thank you, Edwards,' said Mr Butcher. 'I'm sure Face here can answer for himself without your help, can't you, Face? Now, whose form are you in?'

'Same as me, sir,' I interrupted again. '8C. We were just showing him round when you ran into us, sir.'

'Correction, Edwards,' snarled Mr Butcher. 'You ran into me.'

'No, sir. I mean yes, sir. Sorry, sir.'

I was stalling for time. Butch had on the black gown he always wore when he was giving an assembly. That meant he'd be in a hurry to get to the hall before the first classes started to arrive. With a bit of luck, we'd get away with an ear bashing and that'd be the end of it.

I was right. The bell sounded for registration.

Mr Butcher looked at his watch and then at Jean. He even managed a smile.

'Well, Face,' he said, 'saved by the bell this chime, eh?' There was an embarrassing silence. 'Ahem, yes, well I hope you learn something from this little episode, Face. If you take my advice, you'll get to know some of our more mature young people and forget you ever saw this rag, tag and bobtail collection of miscreants.'

I guessed he meant Beaker and me, though who Miss Creant was I couldn't imagine. I was in Mr Norris's form.

Butch was going to be late for assembly. He turned to Beaker.

'Right then, Simpson. Jump to it, lad. I'd hate you to miss registration on one of the rare days you decide to grace us with your presence. Doubtless your two cronies there will remind you how to get to your form room.'

Even Beaker knew better than to argue with Mr Butcher when he was in one of these moods. And besides, he had something much more important on his mind.

'Break-time – the shed,' he muttered as he pushed past me. 'Be there!'

Chapter 11

I hurried Jean off in the opposite direction. I'd already decided Ollie Norris could whistle for registration. It was time Jean and me had a serious talk. In private. When we got level with the door to the boys' loo, I pushed him inside. It seemed as convenient a place as any. We were lucky. Except for the early morning smokescreen, the loo was empty.

'Now,' I said, 'mind telling me what all that was about?'

He held out his hands and shrugged.

'I am not understanding all of it either, Joey. This teacher uses many big words to me – some I am not hearing before. He is saying to meet with more manure young people. What is this manure, please? I am not recognising it.'

'You ought to,' I snapped. 'You're in it up to your neck – or will be when Beaker catches up with you. What d'ye want to go and hit him like that for?'

"Because it is the custom in our country," he said firmly, "like you have your fish and chips in England."

"Yeah," I said, thinking ahead to break-time, "but here it's just the fish as gets battered. And you still haven't said why you hit him."

"I do, Joey, I do," he insisted. He waved his hand through the air. "I say 'This is for the lovely Victoria and this is for Joey.' Then I am being your champion, yes?"

I was beginning to lose patience.

"Champion?" I said. "What d'ye mean 'champion'?"

The only champion I'd ever heard of had four legs and a tail and had probably ended up as dog meat years ago. Talking of which reminded me.

"And will you stop going on about the lovely Victoria all the time. She ain't lovely – she's my sister."

"Exactement, Joey!" he said, suddenly getting all worked up and waving his arms about like he was trying to take off. "You English have a saying, yes? Like brother, like sister. It is true. I am liking the brother and I am liking the sister very much also. When they are insulted, I, Jean Eduarde Claude Boniface, do them the honour of avenging this insult."

"Come again," I said.

"A duel. Man to man. It is the custom."

"A duel?" I looked at him incredulous. "Man to man? You and Beaker Simpson?"

"Of course. Why else am I slapping the Beaky's face?"

There could be any number of reasons, but nothing to touch the one he'd just come up with.

By now he'd stopped doing his whirlybird impression. I grabbed hold of his arms and pinned him against the wall.

"Now you listen to me, Jean," I said, "and listen good. First off, Beaker Simpson has not insulted anyone. All he did was say a few things about our Vicki on account of something she done to annoy him. Secondly, surprising as it may seem to you, we don't go in much for fighting duels and that round here. I don't reckon Beaker Simpson even knows what the word means, let alone that he's supposed to be in one. And thirdly, the best thing you can do for me right now is to leg it and catch the next boat back to France, okay? Go back to Longville or wherever it is and forget you ever saw me – or Beaker Simpson, or our Mam, or Vicki, or Mrs Lewis or Norm's Caff or anything. Just – go – home!"

It was like talking to a brick wall. In fact, as bricks went, I reckoned he was several short of a full load.

"I know why you are doing this, Joey,"

he said, looking all solemn and serious. "You are thinking I am not winning the duel with Beaky Simpson. By saying these things you try to save me from myself. It is most kind. I am touched."

For once I agreed with him.

"You're touched alright," I said. "Touched in the bleedin' head. Beaker Simpson'll marmalise you."

He grinned.

"You do not think perhaps I have something up my sleeves to, as you say, make marmalade of this Beaky?"

I said I didn't care if he had the SAS up one sleeve and half the French Foreign Legion up the other. Beaker Simpson'd still murder him.

"Then you will not help me, Joey?" He looked disappointed. "You will not be my afters against Beaky?"

"Your what?" I said.

Afters were things like rice pudding and apple crumble. I couldn't see the connection, unless he meant that frogspawn stuff with the blob of jam in the middle. In which case, Beaker Simpson probably had something similar in mind.

"My afters," Jean repeated. "It is like in the boxing match, no? When the bell is ringing and they say 'Afters out – round three'."

"It's 'seconds out' you idiot," I said, suddenly realising what he was on about. "Seconds, not afters. And anyway, the answer's no."

He slapped a hand to his forehead.

"Ah so," he said, "I am using the wrong word again. One day my stupidity is making trouble for me, eh, Joey?"

"If you live that long," I said glumly.

I was listening to the bell sounding for the end of registration. Less than two hours and it'd be break-time. The most important thing now was to put as much distance as possible between us and Beaker Simpson. I reckoned about twenty miles would do for starters. Which meant actually getting the pair of us out of the building to begin with.

That's where – or rather, when – Mr Butcher came in.

"Not you two again," he snapped irritably. "What is it this time, Edwards? A guided tour of the little boys' room, or isn't Face here old enough to go on his own?"

I took a couple of steps forward.

"Something like that, sir," I said, thinking quickly. "He's feeling sick, sir. I'm looking after him, sir. Mr Norris said, sir."

It was obvious Butch didn't believe a word of it.

"I'm sick, too, Edwards," he said, "sick of the sight of you wandering round the school all day long and never being where you should be. And as for you, Face." He turned towards Jean. "I'm disappointed in you, boy. Very disappointed. You don't look the sort to –"

Mr Butcher stopped suddenly. He was peering past me, staring intently at Jean. I wheeled round. Jean was leaning against one of the cubicle doors. He was bent almost double and moaning softly to himself. Mr Butcher went to move forward. At which point Jean let out a groan, just loud enough for it to sound convincing. Butch hesitated. I could see he was taken in. Hardly surprising, I suppose. The kid even had me fooled for a moment. Specially when his cheeks puffed out like his mouth was full of something horrible and he made a dash for the cubicle, clutching at his stomach.

Made quite an impression on Mr Butcher that did. Almost as good as the sounds of retching and throwing up that followed. Mr Butcher backed away. He began making the sort of helpful noises teachers make when someone's been sick and they don't want to get mixed up in it, so to speak.

You know the sort of thing.

"Yes, well, er, better get Face cleaned up, Edwards. Then, er, get him down to the Medical Room, I think."

"Yes, sir."

"I suppose he'll need to take the rest of the day off."

"Looks that way, sir."

"Mm. Yes. Well, I'll leave a note in Reception to that effect."

"Yes, sir … Sir?"

Butch looked at his watch.

"Yes, what is it Edwards?"

"Will you be taking him home in your car, sir? He'll probably be alright as long as he keeps his head out the window, sir."

A loud groan from the cubicle was followed by a prolonged silence.

"Ahem, yes, well, I'm glad you brought that up, Edwards."

More groans from the cubicle.

"I suppose someone had better go with him." He looked at his watch again. "It's just that I'm rather –"

"You see, I know where he lives, sir. I could write down the directions for you while you're getting some of them sick bags they keep in the Medical Room, sir."

One more particularly loud groan from Jean clinched it. Ten minutes later, there we were, strolling out of the building as large as life, each with a "Permission to Leave School" pass timed, dated and signed "Mr R. Butcher, Deputy Headteacher".

"Pretty good scam, that," I said, once we were safely back in the land of the living.

I meant it, too. It wasn't often I got the chance to put one over on old Butcher.

Jean's face broke into a grin. He went through the motions of blowing out his cheeks and clutching his stomach so that we both fell about laughing.

We walked on in silence for a bit then, while I considered what to do next. It wasn't easy. Despite the fact that he'd done nothing but cause trouble, I couldn't help feeling somehow responsible for Jean. Well, let's face it, someone had to be. What with one thing and another, the kid was pretty much a walking disaster area. Fortunately it was Monday already, and whatever else happened he'd have to go back on Thursday with the others.

Me, I'd have liked to see him off there and then, but I didn't suppose there was much chance of that. Even if he had the money to get back to France, it wouldn't have been enough. Old Butcher's note might get him out of school – it certainly wouldn't get him out of the country. And Mrs Lewis had kept all the passports on account of she didn't want any of the kids losing them.

So, in the meantime, all I had to do was keep Jean away from Beaker Simpson for a few days, solve the business with his dad's trucks, make my peace with Beaker, smooth it over between him and our Vicki, and find something to explain Face's sudden disappearance from school that old Butcher would swallow. And I still hadn't had a chance to explain to Sharon about the competition and that.

"Oh, well," I thought, putting a hand in my trouser pocket, "things could be worse."

I was right an' all.

"Damn!"

Jean looked up, startled.

"I've only gone and lost the flippin' front door key, haven't I?" I said. "It must have dropped out when I ran into old Butcher. Damn!"

"There is no-one in the house still?" asked Jean, trying to sound helpful.

"No," I said crossly. "Our Vicki's out, and our Mam won't be back till lunch-time. She always goes shopping with me Auntie

Viv Monday mornings."

"And there is no way in? A window perhaps?"

"You must be joking," I said scornfully. "Leave a window open? Round here you count yourself lucky if the house is still there when you get back from the shops. No, our Mam's got it locked tighter than the Bank of England. We'll just have to wait some place else till she gets back."

By which time, of course, Beaker Simpson and his mates would be out looking for us.

"How are we off for spends?" I said. "I've still got the dinner money our Mam gave us."

We stood on the pavement and counted the small collection of coins. It came to about a fiver. Not exactly millionaire stuff but still better than I'd expected. Which just left the problem of where to go. All round those parts was Beaker Simpson territory, and I didn't want to risk bumping into any of his mates who might be wagging school. News travels fast here, and there was no way of knowing how much he'd already let on about him and Jean and our Vicki.

It was the Froggy who came up with the idea.

"Please, Joey," he said quietly. "I should like to be going again with you to Norm's Caff."

Perhaps it was the way he said "please" that did it. That, or the look in his eyes that said he was going anyway.

I shrugged.

"Okay," I said. "Why not?"

It was certainly the last place on earth Beaker or any of his goons would think of looking for us. In fact, health-wise we'd probably be in more danger from the effects of Norm's cooking than anything else. And it would be somewhere to sit and talk.

Chapter 12

We were on our way down the High Street when we met Miss Shepherd. She was coming out of one of those offices you sometimes find sandwiched between two shops. She had a man with her, too, a tall bloke in a dark suit who looked sort of familiar. There was a sign on the door printed in gold block letters – "Turner and Stretton, Solicitors and Commissioners for Oaths".

"Hello, Miss," I said, wondering how come she was there in the first place. It wasn't like Miss Shepherd to wag school.

She turned suddenly.

"Oh, hello, Joey. This is a surprise. What are you doing here?"

That was one of the nice things about Miss Shepherd. None of your "Oh, it's you Edwards. Why aren't you in school, boy?" With her it was a polite friendly greeting, like you were a real person and not just some twerp out of 8C.

All the same, I didn't answer straight off. I was staring at Miss Shepherd. She seemed different somehow. Like as if she was down about something. And I noticed she wasn't wearing any make-up. I glanced up at the man with her, and then back to Miss

Shepherd.

"Everything alright, Miss?" I said. "You look like you been crying or summat."

The bloke in the suit took a step forward. I frowned, trying to remember where I'd seen him before.

"If you'd rather we – " he began, but Miss Shepherd put a hand on his arm and shook her head.

"No, it's alright. Joseph here's one of my pupils. He's going to be a writer when he gets older, aren't you, Joey?"

I shuffled my feet on the pavement and felt this sort of red glow creeping up the back of my neck. The fella in the suit seemed to relax. Miss Shepherd glanced towards Jean and then back to me. She smiled.

"Aren't you going to introduce me to your good-looking friend, Joey," she said.

It was Jean's turn to blush.

"What? Oh, yeah. Sorry, Miss. This here's Jean. He's a Fro… I mean French. Jean's staying with us for a few days. One of them exchange things."

"That must be nice for you, Joey," said Miss Shepherd.

I nodded.

She turned to Jean.

"Comment allez-vous, Jean? Je

m'appele Mademoiselle Shepherd."

Surprised me that did, Miss Shepherd being able to speak French an' all. I suppose because I'd only ever seen her teaching us English. I knew more or less what she was saying, though. One of my French textbooks has this section on "Useful Phrases" that I've had to copy out a few times during detentions. But even that didn't help when it came to following Jean's reply. He lost me completely after the first "Tres bien, merci" bit, but Miss Shepherd seemed to understand all right.

"Your friend seems very nice, Joey," she said when he'd finished. "And he obviously thinks a lot of you, judging from some of the things he's been telling me."

I was tempted to ask what things exactly, but I didn't. All the time they'd been talking, the tall bloke was looking at his watch and shuffling his feet, so I sussed it was probably time we were off. I nudged Jean.

"Come on," I said. "We'd better be going. Mr Butcher said as how I was to get you straight home, remember. Jean's been sick, you see, Miss," I added by way of explanation.

Miss Shepherd looked surprised.
"Oh, I am sorry to hear that, Jean.

Well, I'm sure Joey here will look after you." She held out her hand. "I don't suppose I'll see you again before you go. I hope you enjoy the rest of your stay with us."

They shook hands.

Miss Shepherd leaned over towards me.

"And you make sure you've done your homework by the time I come back, young man," she said playfully. "No excuses, mind. You'll have had a full week. And no bad reports about my star pupil from whoever's taking my lessons. Okay?"

I nodded.

There was a pause.

"Are you going to be away from school for long, then, Miss?" I said.

She managed a smile but I could see there was something wrong.

"A few days at least, Joey. Certainly until the end of the week." She hesitated. "You see, my mother died last week and … well … let's just say there have been one or two complications."

"Aw, Miss, I'm sorry. I wouldn't have said anything if – "

"Don't worry, Joey," she said. It's fine. Just fine." She gave a short laugh. "In fact, it's quite a tonic seeing you and Jean here.

What with running around making arrangements for the funeral and dealing with the police, I'd almost forgotten school existed."

It suddenly twigged then, her mentioning the police and that. I knew I'd seen the fella in the suit somewhere before. In fact it was the clothes that had thrown me. Last time I'd seen him, he was standing in front of the fire all dripping wet in his uniform and telling our Mam as how he'd fished me out of the ornamental fountain.

Miss Shepherd must have read the expression on my face. She laughed.

"That's right, Joey," she said, "this gentleman is Detective Sergeant Parry. I've been assisting him with some enquiries he's making."

I frowned.

"You're not in any trouble are you, Miss?"

This time they both laughed. Miss Shepherd turned to this Detective Parry bloke.

"I think you'd better tell them, Alan," she said. "Otherwise it'll be all round school that I've been arrested or something." She paused, and then added, "I take it you and Joseph have met before?"

"In a manner of speaking," he said with a wide grin. "Let's just say we both enjoy a spot of fishing now and again, and leave it at that, eh, Joey?"

I hadn't realised coppers could have a sense of humour. I began to like Detective Parry. Besides, Miss Shepherd must have thought he was okay or she wouldn't have been helping him like she said.

"It's rather a long story," said Detective Parry. "I suggest we all go across the road for a hot drink so that Jean here can sit down out of the cold. Agreed?"

I nodded enthusiastically. Apart from wanting to hear what he had to say, I reckoned we'd be safe even from the likes of Beaker Simpson with Miss Shepherd and Detective Parry for company.

It was still early, and the restaurant was almost deserted. A waitress showed us to a table, disappeared with our order, and returned almost at once with two cups of coffee and a couple of hot chocolates for Jean and me. Bit of a difference from Norm's, I thought, noting her smart uniform and the careful way she placed the cups and saucers down on the immaculate white linen tablecloth.

"Well, to begin with, lads," Detective

Parry said when the waitress had gone, "you can take it from me that Julie here, or rather Miss Shepherd, isn't in any kind of trouble. Not the sort of trouble you mean, any way. What she is doing is trying to help us catch whoever's behind a particularly unpleasant series of burglaries that have been taking place recently." He glanced at Miss Shepherd and smiled. "That's right, isn't it, Julie?"

She nodded.

"Aw, Miss, you ain't been burgled as well, have you?" I said.

What with that and the death of her Mam, it was no wonder she didn't look too good.

Miss Shepherd lowered the coffee cup and shook her head slowly.

"No, not me, Joey," she said with a sigh. "Although I almost wish it had been me instead of …"

Her voice trailed off. Detective Parry leaned and put an arm round her shoulder. He murmured something I couldn't catch and then straightened up. I stared hard at the cup on the table and felt suddenly uncomfortable. I guessed Jean was much the same. I was glad when Detective Parry started in again.

"You've probably realised by now that it's Julie's mum's house we're talking about here."

I nodded.

"That's what makes this case, and the others, particularly nasty," he went on. "The thief or thieves – we think there must be a gang of them – seem to specialise in doing houses where someone has died recently. Usually where the person was elderly and had been living on their own – a widow or widower, for example. They've obviously sussed that when the person dies, it's likely the house will be empty for a few days or so while the relatives sort out what they're going to do with it. That's when they make their move. They force an entry, nick what valuables they can, and leave. And no-one's the wiser until the deceased's relatives arrive to open up the house again. Which may not be for days – especially if the person's family are living away from Birmingham." He paused and his eyes narrowed. "I reckon as we've got every copper in the city on the look-out – uniform, under cover, the lot – but it doesn't make for an easy crime to solve, as you can probably imagine."

"Mon dieu!" Jean exclaimed suddenly. "It is despicable. That such men exist!"

"You're right, son, it is despicable. But they do exist, believe me. Julie's here brings the number of cases up to a dozen at least. There are probably others that we haven't even heard about. Down at the station we call the men we're after 'The Grave-Robbers' because what they do is a bit like robbing the dead, if you see what I mean."

"But how do they know when someone's died?" I asked.

"Easier than you think, Joey," replied Detective Parry. "The newspaper's as good a place as any. In those columns where they announce things like births, marriages and deaths."

Of course, I'd even read through some of them a couple of times myself when I was bored and there was nothing else to read. But surely they didn't print people's addresses there as well. That would be a dead giveaway.

There was a pause and then they all three burst out laughing. Even Miss Shepherd, which I couldn't fathom until Detective Parry explained.

"A dead giveaway. I like that. If it weren't so serious it would be really funny, that would."

He repeated the phrase again to himself and chuckled.

I still wasn't sure I really understood

what he was on about. But at least I'd helped to cheer them all up, and that was something.

"I told you he was sharp, Alan," Miss Shepherd said approvingly. "And you're right, Joey," she went on, "they don't print the addresses in the newspapers. But once the thieves have got a name to go on, it's just a matter of looking up the address on the internet or on the list of people who are eligible to vote."

I knew about that – the electoral roll they call it. I'd seen a copy of it a couple of times in the library when I'd gone with Little Mo to meet his Mam from work.

Jean, who'd been following the conversation with some interest, looked up.

"Yes, but how are they knowing when the house is empty?"

"Good question, Jean," said Detective Parry. "We think they quite simply watch the place. It's not difficult in a city this big with so many people and cars around all the time. And don't forget, we're dealing with a bunch of experts here, much as I hate having to say it. They're organised, they've obviously got transport, and they know exactly what to take. They're also very confident," he added. "In at least two cases it seems they've actually knocked off the house while the relatives have been attending the funeral."

"In broad daylight?"

"In broad daylight, Joey. You wouldn't credit it, would you?"

I shook my head.

"Now perhaps you can understand why we're so anxious to find whoever's responsible and see to it that they're put away for a good long stretch. Which is where Julie here comes in."

"I'm afraid I'm not being much help," Miss Shepherd said apologetically.

Detective Parry squeezed her arm gently.

"At least you were able to contact us the morning after the robbery," he said, trying to reassure her. "And you were able to give us a detailed list of all the missing items. Which means we know what we're looking for. That's a start – and a good one. In most cases we've been working in the dark, as it were. Mainly because the relatives haven't really known what the old lady or gentleman had stashed away in the house to begin with."

Miss Shepherd sighed and nodded her head.

"Thanks, Alan," she said. "I didn't mean to sound depressed. It's just that I wish

I could do more. As it is, I only knew what was missing because Mother wanted to change some of her insurance policies a few months back. I helped her compile a list of everything that needed to be covered. Otherwise, I wouldn't have had a clue. I never dreamt that one day the list would be in a police file under 'Stolen Property'." Her voice began to falter. "If only I hadn't put that damn notice in the paper. I could kick myself."

"Don't blame yourself, Julie," Detective Parry said quietly. "You weren't to know, and anyway, chances are they'd have found out sooner or later. The important thing now is to catch them before too many other innocent people get hurt."

Miss Shepherd took a small packet of tissues from her handbag. She peeled one off and used it to dab her eyes.

I finished the last of my hot chocolate and gave Jean the wink that it was probably time we were off. Seeing Miss Shepherd upset like that had given me an idea.

"Have you got one of them lists, Miss?" I said. "You know, with all the stuff from your Mam's house on it."

Detective Parry guessed straight-off what I was up to.

"Several," he said. "We had it typed up

at the station and then photocopied to send round different places. That's where we'd been when we met you pair." He nodded over his shoulder towards the office doorway across the road. "Julie's solicitor needed a copy. Now I suppose you two want one as well so's you can play detective, eh?"

"Well ... we would like to help Miss Shepherd," I said, hesitating in case she didn't think it was a good idea. "And we could look out for stuff in second-hand shops and the market and that – on our way to and from school, of course," I added quickly.

Detective Parry thought for a moment, then reached inside his jacket pocket. He pulled out a sheet of official-looking paper, neatly folded. He glanced at us, then at Miss Shepherd, as if to say 'Well, what do you think?' She shrugged her shoulders and smiled.

"Go on, Alan," she said. "What harm can it do? They're on our side ... and you never know. Joey's a sensible lad, and I'm sure it'll give Jean something to talk about when he gets back to France."

Detective Parry held out the list. I took it and put it safely in my pocket.

"Thanks, Miss," I said. "We'll let you know if we find anything."

Jean and me walked on down the High Street a bit before I stopped and looked back. Miss Shepherd and Detective Parry had crossed over the road and were getting into a car. He was holding open the passenger door, and I noticed the way he took her arm to help her in. It felt good seeing the two of them like that together. Sort of natural. Funny thing was, I didn't mind – about him being a copper, I mean. Something told me he'd be taking mighty fine care not to let anything else upset Miss Shepherd from now on.

Chapter 13

"I like your Miss Shepherd very much," Jean said. "She is a fine lady."

We were sitting at the same table as on our previous visit to Norm's. You could still make out the sticky ring where Jean had rested his can of Coke.

The caff was as dismal as ever, and if anything, seemed smaller than I remembered it. Probably because there were more people in it this time round. Lorry drivers most of them, judging from the assortment of trucks parked outside, a couple of student hitch-hikers, and finally the wino sitting on his own again just inside the doorway. At least he seemed a bit more awake this time. Though from the way he was swigging a bottle of something wrapped in brown paper, I didn't give much for his chances of seeing it through to lunch-time even.

"Yeah, she's all right is Miss Shepherd," I said absent-mindedly. I was staring at Jean's plate. "You gonna eat that?"

We'd ordered two mugs of soup and Jean had asked for a round of bacon sarnies. Using both hands, he picked one of them up and held it out. The sarnie dripped grease all down his fingers.

"You want us to share, Joey? There is plenty to be going round."

"No fear! It's your funeral," I said, and then wished I hadn't. It made me think of Miss Shepherd and how upset she'd been over what had happened to her old girl.

I fished out the list Detective Parry had given us and glanced through it while Jean polished off the sarnies in double quick time. Surprised me it did, seeing him eat stuff like that. I'd always thought the French were particular about their food.

Detective Parry's list was longer than I'd expected. I couldn't fathom all the words – especially the descriptions of some of the jewellery – but most of it was clear enough. Rings, brooches, watches – the usual sort of thing. Oh, and a couple of paintings – miniatures, whatever that meant – by some foreign bloke I'd never heard of. Typed against each article was the price, or rather, what the thing was insured for. I did a quick bit of mental arithmetic.

"Phew!"

Jean looked up from his plate.

"You are finding something interesting, Joey?"

"You could say that," I said. "Guess what this little lot comes to when you add it all up?"

He shrugged.

"I do not know, but I am thinking perhaps it is much money."

I stared him straight in the face.

"You're not kidding! Give or take the odd pound, those guys ripped off over fifty thousand quids' worth of stuff. Fifty grand! Would you believe it?"

Knock off all the houses in our street and I didn't reckon you'd get that much worth of stuff from the whole lot of them.

Looking back over the list, I noticed something else as well. Not only were the different articles worth a mint. One fella could have carted off the lot in a decent-sized suitcase and still had room for a flask and his butty-box.

"And there are many men carrying suitcases at the airports and railway stations, I am thinking," Jean muttered.

"You reckon that's why the coppers never get a lead on the stuff?" I said. "Because the 'Grave Robbers' as old Parry called them move it out of town as … "

Jean kicked me hard under the table.

"Norm," he whispered.

Instinctively I shoved the list back in my pocket.

I was sitting with my back to the counter and didn't see Norm till he leaned across the table to pick up Jean's empty plate. He glanced at the barely-touched mugs of soup and scowled.

"Shouldn't you kids be in school?" he muttered sourly.

Fag ash from the cigarette dangling in the corner of his mouth fell onto the table.

Close up, the thing you noticed was his eyes. Shifty they were, always on the move – looking, watching, never missing a trick – so that you got to thinking they were a bit like Norm's Caff itself: they never closed, not even when he slept.

"We're on a field trip," I lied. "Doing a survey of local shops and that. Just nipped in for a minute while the teacher wasn't watching."

He wasn't amused. Leastways not so it showed. He gave a sort of grunt and made his way back to the counter, pausing to exchange a few words with the wino.

Jean's watch was showing almost eleven thirty, later than I thought. We must have been talking with Miss Shepherd and Detective Parry for ages. Another hour and school would break for lunch, which meant Beaker Simpson would be out looking for us.

I reckoned our Mam would be back from shopping with Auntie Viv about the same time. If we got a move on, we might just make it home before Beaker made the place a no-go area.

It was only a temporary solution, of course. I couldn't keep Jean locked up in the house right through till Thursday. Sooner or later, Beaker Simpson would have to be faced. I'd settle for later.

Besides, I had a feeling there was more to this particular trip to Norm's than just a craving for bacon sarnies. I'd noticed the way Jean had eyeballed the various lorries on our way in, like he was looking for one in particular. No prizes for guessing which one, of course. And it was the same on our way out.

"No luck?" I said as we reached the main road.

He shrugged and I could see he was disappointed.

"Never mind," I began, "maybe you ..."

Jean wasn't listening. He was too busy watching a huge container lorry that had emerged from a side street some fifty metres away. The moment the truck turned into Norm's, Jean was off and running, back across the car park.

Even at that distance, I could see the truck was foreign. A bit closer and I could make out the words MUNICH – PARIS – LONDON along one side. There was nothing to identify it as one of Mr Boniface's trucks, however.

Jean was already talking to the driver when I strolled across. Turned out the driver was French, too, which made it impossible to follow what they were on about. I stood and waited. Funny lot, the French, when they're talking to one another. All sort of loud and excited, and they use their hands more than we do so that it wears you out just watching them. Anyway, this went on for a few minutes before the driver opened the door of his cab again and climbed back inside.

Jean came and stood beside me. At least he seemed happy enough.

"Do not be looking so worried, Joey. This man is understanding our little problem and is willing to help us if he is able."

"Oh yeah?" I said.

"Little problem" was hardly the phrase I'd have used to describe Beaker Simpson. And how could some French lorry driver I'd never seen before possibly help? Unless, that is, Jean could talk the fella into giving him a free ride home. There would still be the matter of his passport, of course, but maybe he could get round that by hiding in the back of the lorry.

An even better solution would be for the driver to take Beaker Simpson back to France, and manage to lose him somewhere – like in the middle of the English Channel, for instance. Now that really would be a help.

I was still mulling over the idea when the driver leant out of the cab, pointing to his mobile phone. He was all smiles and gave a thumbs up sign.

Jean gave a little whoop of delight.

"Alors, c'est merveilleux!" he said excitedly. "It is our lucky day, Terry."

"Yeah," I said through gritted teeth. "Glad you think so."

I looked on as the driver climbed down and locked the cab. He said something to Jean which made the pair of them laugh, and strolled off in the direction of the caff.

Well, one thing was certain. Whatever else they'd been cooking up together, it didn't involve smuggling Jean, or anyone else for that matter, across the Channel and into France. Which meant we'd spent the best part of three hours doing everything but solve the problem of how to keep Jean out of Beaker Simpson's way until Thursday.

To tell the truth, he didn't seem particularly concerned. I could see he was itching to tell me whatever it was had chuffed him so much, but I made him wait. There wasn't time, leastways not until we'd legged it up the road and were safely aboard a number fifty-two bus which would drop us off just round the corner from our house.

Downstairs was crowded with wrinklies using their free passes. Upstairs, though, we had the place more or less to ourselves, so it was okay to talk.

Odd that, the way we got sort of secretive if other people were around. Like as if we didn't want them to hear. It'd been the same in Norm's Caff – whispering to each other, and my not wanting Norm sneaking a look at Detective Parry's list of stolen property.

It was getting so we weren't quite sure who to trust any longer, which in a way was a good thing 'cos it brought us closer together. They say that a trouble shared is a trouble halved, and in our case it seemed we had more than enough to go round – plus a few to spare thrown in for good measure. And it was still only Monday morning remember.

Chapter 14

As it was, this new spirit of Anglo-French accord nearly came to an abrupt end there and then on the top deck of the number fifty-two. It was just after we'd turned into Catherine Street and Jean began outlining his plan for the rest of the day – or rather, for that evening to be precise.

"Give over," I said. "Who d'ye think we are, Batman and Robin? Besides, our Mam'd never let us out the house if she knew."

"I know this," he said, nodding his head. "And I do not like lying to Mrs Edwards as much as you do, Joey, but this time it seems we must."

"What's all this 'we' business?" I snapped back.

I was getting a bit fed up of being included in whatever scam he had in mind without even so much as a please or thank you. It was exactly this sort of inconsiderate way of going about things that had landed us in the mess with Beaker Simpson to begin with.

And that was another reason for calling a halt before matters started to get complicated, which, if Jean had anything to do with them, was a sure-fire certainty.

"You don't think Beaker's just going to let you come and go as you please, do you?" I said. "He'll have our house watched like it's 10 Downing Street or somewhere. Nobody'll get in or out without he knows about it in ten seconds flat."

Jean pursed his lips and stared out of the window.

"Perhaps I should go to see Beaky," he said suddenly. "Explain that I am not wanting to, how you say, 'chicken out' of the duel, but only to be putting it back a little. Perhaps then he will listen. I do not think he is unreasonable."

"No, he's not unreasonable," I said sarcastically. "He'll listen – and then he'll rip yer head off. Let's face it, Jean, there ain't no way we can get out of the house tonight and not run into Beaker Simpson or some of his mates."

Jean shook his head.

"No," he said firmly. "It must be tonight."

I could see there was no point in arguing. Short of my tying him to the bed or telling our Mam what he was up to, Jean was going back to Norm's Caff – Beaker Simpson or no Beaker Simpson.

It was our Vicki who brought the message from Beaker.

She was so excited, she came barging straight into my room, completely forgetting it was a no-go area to big sisters as laid down by the Joseph Edwards Convention on Human Rights and Civil Liberties. A split second later and she'd have had a neat little hole between the eyes where my dart would have landed, on account of it was heading straight for treble twenty till she opened the door. Instead of which, the dart took a deflection off the edge of the door, nose-dived, and did a perfect kamikaze job on a plastic football in the corner of the room.

"Joey!" she exclaimed. "You know you're not supposed to play darts in the bedroom. Our Mam said."

Thing was, our Mam had popped next door for a chat, and I was using the opportunity to teach Jean the finer points of "Killer!" and "180!"

"Just helping the condemned man while away his last few hours," I said, squashing the deflated ball into a shape that reminded me of our Vicki's face.

I didn't suppose for a minute she needed any explanation. Our Vicki had ears like Dumbo the Elephant, and anyway it'd be all round the street what had happened. She was also wearing one of those looks that girls put on when they think they know something you don't. And for once she was right. Well, they say the exception proves the rule.

"Point is, you can relax," she said. "I've just seen that idiot Beaker Simpson and he says to tell you it's off for the time being. Something's come up apparently."

It certainly had. Our lucky number, if what our Vicki'd said was true.

"Only for the time being, though," she repeated, clocking the way I was suddenly all smiles again. "He says to tell you same time, same place, Wednesday. He says he'd have told you himself but he thinks you're too scared to come out of the house. And he isn't going to school tomorrow 'cos he doesn't want them to think he's going soft on the place by showing up two days running. So there."

She paused and took a deep breath.

"Oh, and there's something else."

"Oh yeah?" I said suspiciously. I knew our Vicki had a nasty habit of keeping the bad news till last.

She walked over and stood in front of Jean.

"This," she said, and she put her arms

round his neck and kissed him.

A real smacker it was, too, full on the lips and without so much as a warning, so that the poor kid didn't even get a chance to defend himself.

I don't know who was more shocked, him or me. I reckon it was probably him, though, on account of he was the injured party, whereas I just happened to be an innocent bystander. Paralysed him it did an' all, which would explain how come he didn't seem able to stop her.

Worse was to follow.

Our Vicki looked him straight in the eyes.

"I think what you're doing is the nicest, bravest, most romantic thing anybody has ever done in the whole wide world," she said. "I want you to know that whatever happens, I shall never forget what you did or why you did it, and I want you to have this."

She fished in her blazer pocket and brought out this bit of black wispy stuff with frills round the edges.

"Wear it for me," she breathed, all sort of deep and husky like.

I suppose she was trying to make Jean feel more at home by imitating the women in those soppy French films where you have to read the subtitles to know what's going on. "Mon sherry," and all that sort of thing. Except that when our Vicki tried, it made her sound like a whale coming up for air.

I could see Jean was embarrassed. And as for me, well, I was falling about at the thought of him wearing one of our Vicki's scrunchies. I mean, they're okay for putting round your head when you're a little kid playing Cowboys and Indians. They even make reasonable catapults if you're pushed. But they weren't exactly the sort of thing any self-respecting lad was likely to tie up his hair with, always assuming that he had long enough hair to begin with.

I suppose Jean only took it 'cos he didn't want to go upsetting our Vicki, him being a guest and that. He whispered something to her in French that sounded like "jet aim" and which I took to mean "Ta very much", or words to that effect.

Our Vicki seemed pleased enough anyway. She was still smiling when she came over to where I was standing with the tears rolling down my face.

"And I've got something for you as well, our Joey," she said, keeping one hand behind her back like she was hiding summat.

"Oh yeah?" I said, thinking it was another message from Beaker, or maybe even from Sharon who I hadn't seen for a couple of days. "What?"

"This!"

I was right about her hiding something behind her back. It was her fist. And coming from that distance and at that speed, it hurt I can tell you. Knocked me clean on the floor it did.

"That," she said triumphantly, "is for not looking after Jean here properly and for getting him into trouble with Beaker Simpson. And this –" she kicked me hard across the shins – "this is for me, for calling me all those horrid names."

It was an English variation on the old one-two that Jean had tried out on Beaker Simpson. Obviously it was catching on fast. Assuming I would ever walk again, it might be something worth practising.

I was still picking myself up off the floor when she left. I tried putting a brave face on it on account of no-one likes to admit being beaten-up by their big sister.

"And you can wipe that silly grin off yer face an' all," I said. "You don't look so clever yerself standing there with our Vicki's hair band hanging out yer trouser pocket."

"I am just thinking," he said, still grinning from ear to ear, "of what we said earlier, you and me, Joey. About keeping tricks up our sleeves with which we are beating the Beaky."

"Oh yeah?" I said, examining the damage where our Vicki had stuck the boot in.

"Yes," he said, "perhaps it is the lovely Victoria we shall be needing. She does, as you say," – and his eyes positively twinkled – "pack one hell of a punch!"

"Yeah," I said savagely. "Knockout."

Chapter 15

Conning our Mam into letting us out of the house for the evening was easier than I imagined. I suppose because I was so used to her saying "No" all the time whenever I wanted to do something. Which is why I expected her to do the same when Jean asked if it was all right for me and him to go to the cinema.

"It is a new film, Mrs Edwards," I heard him explain, "and a very good one I am thinking. It will be of great help to my English and I am sure Mrs Lewis would be agreeing."

Watching him soft-soap our Mam while he was helping her with the washing-up, I remembered something Beaker had said. About him chatting up our Vicki and that. What with Mrs Lewis, then our Vicki, the Mam, and even Miss Shepherd, he certainly knew how to smooth his way round the women. Though Miss Shepherd excluded, I can't say I thought much of his taste. All the same, I made up my mind to keep him away from Sharon for the time being. No point in getting her mixed up in things that didn't interest her like long-distance lorries and Beaker Simpson and good-looking, smooth-talking Froggies now was there?

In fact, Jean did such a good job convincing our Mam that for one horrible moment I thought she was going to come with us. She changed her mind, though, when Jean said as how parts of the film were set in the jungle with lots of creepy-crawlies and snakes and things. That's when she suddenly remembered she'd promised to help our Vicki with her field-trip project.

And that's how we left them, our Mam and Vicki. Sitting round the kitchen table sorting through bits of twigs and leaves and stuff, and saying things like they hoped it was a good film and not to be too late back.

It's funny how you remember scenes like that. Specially when you're a long way away and in trouble and you're wondering whether you'll ever make it back home again ...

I can't say I noticed much of the journey into town. Something was bugging me, and I couldn't quite suss what it was. Beaker Simpson's crying off like that struck me as odd, of course. But no, it wasn't that. It had to do with Detective Parry and the business over Miss Shepherd's old girl. I thought about it for a while, and then gave up and concentrated instead on what Jean had planned for the rest of the evening. By doing that, I was hoping whatever I was trying to remember might suddenly come back, you know the way it does sometimes.

Thinking ahead didn't actually help much. To tell the truth, it scared the living daylights out of me.

You see, what Jean had sussed from the Froggy driver was that Michel was in town. Or at least he would be, always assuming Jean had got his calculations right. These were based largely on the principle that what goes up the M6 must come down the M6. Get it? No, neither did I till he explained it.

The point was, Michel's truck had been eyeballed travelling north of Birmingham on the M6 the day before. Chances were, Jean said, he'd be spending most of Monday loading up, before setting off back down the motorway again in the evening. Only this time stopping off at Norm's on the way, of course. Well, that was the theory, anyway. On the practical side, the idea was for us to hang about Norm's in the hope that he did show, and then keep an eye on the truck, just in case.

It was the "just in case" bit that had me worried. Specially when Jean sort of shrugged his shoulders and looked blank when I tackled him about it. Frankly, I couldn't see the point. Let's say this Michel character turned up and we kept an eye on things and nothing happened. What would that prove? Nothing, I reckoned. Or what if what was going to happen happened a couple of miles further on down the motorway? Fat lot of use we'd be then, sitting on a bus halfway home trying to figure out what to tell our Mam about this absolutely fantastic film we hadn't seen.

On the other hand, of course, let's say something did happen at Norm's. You know, something really serious like this gang of fellas turning up with the Crown Jewels and wanting to smuggle them across to France in the back of Michel's truck. What were we supposed to do then? Fight? Run for the police? Throw bacon sarnies at them? As far as I was concerned, we couldn't even deal with Beaker Simpson between the pair of us. And you've heard what our Vicki did – even if it was just a lucky punch that caught me off guard. So what chance would we have against a car load of Brummie heavies if they decided to turn nasty? Which they would, of course.

And finally, what if Michelin Man didn't show up at Norm's after all? Where would that leave Jean then? Up the junction without a truck it seemed.

All of which should tell you that one way and another I didn't think much of Jean's idea. I was still going on about it when we got off the bus. It was dark by then and sort of creepy quiet. Like as if the place was holding its breath, waiting for something to happen.

"I must be mad coming down here like this," I moaned. "Think of all the sensible things we could be doing instead – like helping our Vicki with her project, for instance."

Jean didn't say much all the time I was going on like this. I suppose he thought I was talking a lot on account of being nervous. He was right an' all. I hadn't exactly gone a bundle on Norm's Caff in daylight. At night, the place was positively scary. Not that I let on to Jean, of course. I just sort of kept close to him – in case he got lost in the dark or anything, you understand. And at least he'd remembered to bring a torch, which was more than I'd done.

There were upwards of a dozen or so trucks on the car park when we arrived, but no sign of Michel or the Boniface van. Jean switched off the torch.

"Maybe he's already been and gone

and we missed him," I said.

Meaning, of course, there was still plenty of time to see the film if we really wanted to. Our Mam had even given us the money for a large popcorn each.

Jean obviously wasn't into popcorn.

"I am sorry, Joey," he said quietly. "But you see, I must do this. It is a matter of…"

"Yeah, yeah, I know. You told me before, remember? Only this time it's different. If this Michel bloke really is mixed up in something, then the chances are it's for real. So do me a favour, will yer? Whatever happens, just forget the hero bit and keep yer hands in yer pockets. Both of 'em!"

I saw his teeth flash white in the darkness.

"You are meaning to be careful, I am thinking, Joey," he said.

"Oh, I mean to be very careful," I said, working on the principle that I didn't fancy being something our Vicki happened to dig up on one of her future field trips.

The caff itself was busy. There was even a queue to be served. When it was our turn, Norm didn't exactly look pleased to see us. The feeling was mutual.

"What is it this time?" he snarled, in between pouring two mugs of tea.

"Homework?"

I deliberately put the two £1 coins right where he'd slopped the tea.

"Yeah," I said, "something like that."

Norm's weasel eyes narrowed.

"Just so long as it don't become a habit," he said sullenly. "I don't want hordes of kids coming down here upsetting the regular customers, right?"

I was going to say something about his food having much the same effect, but thought better of it. He probably wouldn't have understood anyway.

We found an empty table and I went to sit down. Jean frowned and glanced towards the chair on the opposite side, meaning of course that I should have that one. He seemed nervous all of a sudden, and it was a few seconds before I sussed what he was on about. Of course, Jean wouldn't want to sit facing the door in case Michel came in and recognised him. That would ruin everything.

It also left me with the job of look out. Not that I really minded, 'cept that it would help if I knew what, or rather who, I was looking out for. I didn't suppose for one minute that this Michel character was going to come in wearing a beret with a string of onions round his neck and whistling the

Marseilleise all at the same time.

Jean's face broke into a wide grin. I think it was the first time either of us had smiled all evening.

"You will be knowing Michel, I think," he said hoarsely. We were back to talking in whispers. "He is the largest of all my father's drivers – which is explaining how he can load and unload the van without help. A very large man, yes."

Even so, it didn't seem much to go on. Specially as – with the exception of Norm and the wino – everyone else in the place looked as big as the side of a house anyway.

The wino interested me.

Asleep over his usual table, with his head on his arms, he didn't look like he'd moved much all day. Which was odd in a way, 'cos Norm's was hardly the most comfortable place on earth. And there was something else. Something about the way he slept with his head at just the right angle, so that if he opened his eyes a fraction he could see anyone and everyone who entered or left the place. I thought at first I was imagining it, but the longer I watched him, the more obvious it became …

Like the time when the door opened and Heavy Breather and the Gorilla came in.

I must have reacted pretty sharpish, too, if the look on Jean's face was anything to go by. I shook my head.

"Heavy Breather and the Gorilla," I muttered.

Jean nodded and peered cautiously round.

He was just in time to see the pair of them disappearing behind the counter and through the plastic curtain into the back room where Norm had his kitchen. And if it hadn't been for the fact that they'd had to wait a moment for Norm to lift up the counter flap, I'd have probably missed it.

The newspaper, I mean. Rolled up and sticking out of Heavy Breather's overcoat pocket. I couldn't see which paper it was or anything like that, but it didn't matter.

What did matter was that I'd suddenly remembered what had been bugging me all that time. It was something Detective Parry had said about the "grave robbers" as he called them and how they got their information about which houses to hit.

"Easier than you think, Joey," was how he'd put it. "The newpaper's as good a place as any. In those columns where they announce things like births, marriages and deaths …"

Of course! That was the page Norm, Heavy Breather and the Gorilla had been looking at with such interest on Saturday afternoon. You remember, the time when I'd made the excuse about the footy match. Which also explained why I thought they might have been looking for an exercise bike for Heavy Breather. All the adverts for that sort of thing tend to be on the same pages as the Announcements.

It didn't explain anything else, of course, leastways not yet. But it was a start, and that was more than Detective Parry had.

I thought fast.

If I could get hold of a copy of Saturday's paper and find the right page, there was bound to be a clue there somewhere. Else why would Norm and the others have bothered copying out whatever it was they'd seen?

We don't usually have a local evening paper in our house. Not unless it has something wrapped in it, anyway. And I didn't reckon on Norm lending me his copy, which left Little Mo. I could always leg it round to his place first thing in the morning before school, 'cept that by then it might be too late. In fact, the more I thought about it, the more convinced I was that it would be too late.

Norm, Heavy Breather and the Gorilla were planning a job for that very night. I was sure of it. Everything added up. They'd seen the announcement of someone's death in Saturday's paper, which probably meant the person had died a couple of days before at least. And if what Detective Parry had said was right, the gang would want to move in on the house almost immediately. Chances were, they hadn't knocked it off over the weekend, or he'd have mentioned it. Instead of which he'd been going on about how Miss Shepherd's case was the most recent one.

So then, it had to be that night. Which didn't exactly give us much time to find Detective Parry and tip him off.

One thing was certain. We couldn't just sit around in Norm's half the night on the off chance this Michel character would turn up. Jean wouldn't like it, of course, but that was his problem. This was much more important.

I leaned over the table.

"We're going," I hissed. "Now!"

Startled, he looked up. I was already on my feet.

"No buts," I said. "I'll explain outside."

For once, he didn't argue. We left the mugs of tea where they were and went out into the car park. The wind had got up and it was threatening to rain. I waited for my eyes to adjust to the pitch black, then led Jean round to the side of one of the trucks where it was more sheltered. I wasn't taking any chances. The truck hid us from view of the caff. More important still, it meant we couldn't be overheard.

I told him briefly what was on my mind and why we had to find Detective Parry as soon as possible.

"Three men reading a newspaper," he said quietly when I'd finished. "It is not much to be going on, Joey," and he shrugged. "Many men read newspapers …"

"Yeah, but these aren't just any three men, are they?" I insisted. "Let's face it. One on his own looks bad enough. Put all three together and you could make a whole 'Crimewatch' programme around them, I reckon."

"Perhaps." He didn't sound convinced.

I was anxious to be off and we were wasting time. Any minute now and the gang could be on their way to wherever it was they planned knocking off. And I still had the problem of how to get in touch with Detective Parry. I didn't fancy just walking into any old cop shop. They'd only start asking awkward questions which would waste more time, and then they probably wouldn't believe me anyway. Besides, I still hadn't forgotten that little episode with P.C. Plod outside the footy ground on Saturday afternoon. For all I knew, he'd have had identikit pictures of the pair of us put up in every cop shop in Brum.

    That's when I hit on the idea of phoning Miss Shepherd.

Chapter 16

I shone Jean's torch over the list of stolen property. We were in luck. Miss Shepherd's name appeared at the top as next-of-kin, together with her phone number. Now all I needed was to find a public telephone that worked on account of as usual I didn't have any credit left on the mobile. I could remember seeing one over the road, about a hundred metres up from Norm's.

I told Jean what I was doing, and set off across the car park before he even had a chance to reply. To be honest, at the time I wasn't much bothered whether he came or not. The only thing that mattered was getting to that phone and contacting Detective Parry. There was no door on the box, but the phone itself was working. I put 60p in the slot, dialled the number, and prayed that she hadn't decided on an evening out somewhere. Miss Shepherd's voice answered immediately, almost as if she'd been expecting a call.

"544328."

"Miss Shepherd? Miss Shepherd, it's me, joey Edwards. Miss Shepherd? Is Detective Parry there, Miss Shepherd?"

"No, I'm afraid he isn't. Who is this,

please?"

She obviously hadn't heard me properly.

"Oh, sorry, Miss. It's me, Miss. Out of 8C," I added, just in case.

"Why, Joey, this is a surprise," she said, sounding like she meant it. "Is anything wrong?"

"No, Miss. Leastways not yet. But there will be if I don't get a message to Detective Parry in time for him to catch 'em, Miss."

"Catch who, Joey?"

"Heavy Breather and the Gorilla, Miss."

"Who?"

"Heavy Breather and the Gorilla. Leastways that's what we call them, Miss. Don't know their real names, but Detective Parry'll know who they are when we describe them. They hang around with this other bloke, Norm, who runs a tranny caff down near the motorway, only he's in on it too, on account of we saw the three of them reading the paper together on Saturday and …"

"Slow down a bit, Joey," Miss Shepherd said kindly. "I'm not quite sure I understand all this. Perhaps you'd better start at the beginning."

"There isn't time, Miss," I said anxiously. "Heavy Breather and the Gorilla are all ready to go …"

"Go where, Joey?"

"Dunno, Miss. But if you tell Detective Parry to meet us at Norm's right away and to bring a copy of Saturday's local paper with him …"

"Detective Parry's a very busy man, Joseph. Assuming I was able to get a message to him, I don't think he'd take very kindly to having his time wasted, you know."

It was her teacher's voice. The one she used in the classroom to indicate that things had gone just far enough and it was maybe time people settled down and started acting sensibly. Right now, it also meant she probably didn't believe much of what I'd been telling her and there was no way she was going to contact Detective Parry – leastways not until it was too late.

I reckon if it had been anyone other than Miss Shepherd, I'd have put the phone down there and then. I mean, apart from the fact that it was nothing to do with me anyway, I was the one getting cold and fed-up when I could have been at home or sitting in the cinema enjoying a popcorn.

Miss Shepherd must have guessed

what I was thinking.

"Are you still there, Joseph?" she said quietly.

"Yeah," I said.

"Listen, then. I'm going to ask you a couple of questions. You don't have to answer them if you don't want to, in which case I shall put the phone down and forget we ever had this conversation." There was a pause. "But if you do answer, I want you to tell me the truth. Agreed?"

"Yes, Miss. And then will you get Detective Parry for me, Miss?"

"Yes, Joseph. I promise."

"Ta, Miss. Miss?"

"Yes, Joseph?"

"You won't regret it, Miss. Honest."

She laughed – a sort of chuckle really that meant we were friends again.

"All right, Joey. Now remember, you needn't answer if you don't want to."

The suspense was killing me. I was trying to remember how many minutes you got for your 60p, given that we'd already been talking for what seemed like ages. Miss Shepherd's voice came through again, more sort of quiet and serious this time.

"I assume that when you say 'we', Joey, you mean you and Jean. Am I right?"

"Yes, Miss."

"And that you want me to contact Alan – Detective Parry – because you think you've discovered something in connection with what we were discussing this morning."

"Yes, Miss."

There was a pause while she thought it over. When she spoke again, her voice was calm but firm.

"All right, Joey. I'll see what I can do. No promises, mind," she added quickly. "I'll make sure Detective Parry gets your message as soon as possible, and then it will be up to him to decide what to do. Where did you say you were phoning from again?"

"Norm's," I said. "Norm's Caff. He'll know where it is. Tell him Jean an' me'll be waiting by the phone box across the road."

An element of doubt crept into Miss Shepherd's voice.

"Don't you think you'd be better going home, Joey? It's not a very nice night to be out, and it could take some time for Detective Parry to reach you. I'm sure he …"

"It's okay, Miss," I said quickly. I could just imagine our Mam's face if we suddenly turned up and said as how we were expecting this detective fella round later for supper. "We don't mind waiting. Honest."

"In which case I'd better let you go, so that I can start trying to track Alan down for you. I know he's on duty, but he may have been called out somewhere. Anyway, don't worry. They'll know at the station how to contact him." She ended on a more cautionary note. "And you be careful, young man. That goes for Jean, too."

"Yes, Miss," I said.

"I mean it, Joey. No heroics. I don't want to come back to school and find my star pupil missing."

I got sort of embarrassed then and put the phone down without remembering to say thank you or goodbye even.

Chapter 17

By the time I made it back to the car park, it was starting to rain. Jean had disappeared. Or rather he'd moved. I eventually found him, more by accident than design, crouched by the rear wheel of a petrol tanker that must have just pulled in. The engine was still making those sort of tick-tick noises the way engines do when they're cooling down.

He heard me coming and put a finger up to his lips. I dropped down beside him. Jean motioned with his hands and pointed. I nodded. Poking my head out just far enough round the tanker, I peered through the rain. The truck in question was parked on its own well away from the others on the far side of the car park. In the dark and at that distance, it was impossible to make out any details, but the look on Jean's face said it all.

"Michel?" I whispered.

Jean nodded and pointed towards the caff.

"How long?"

"Three, maybe four minutes."

"What about Heavy Breather and the Gorilla? They still in there?"

"Yes. I am not seeing them leave."

It was even better than I'd dared hope. At least I'd done my bit. The rest was down to Detective Parry.

I straightened up.

"Okay," I said. "So far so good. Now what?"

He shrugged.

"I think we are waiting and seeing, Joey. But I am understanding if you cannot …"

"It's alright by me," I said quickly, "leastways for a while. Miss Shepherd says she'll tell Detective Parry, and that we're to wait until he arrives."

It wasn't exactly word for word, but I didn't want to bore him with too many details.

Jean caught hold of my arm.

"Thank you, Joey," he said. "I am not forgetting this kindness."

"Yeah, well," I said, remembering some of the odd ways he had of showing his gratitude, "how about we get under some cover? I'm getting soaked here."

He nodded and pulled up the hood of his anorak.

"Yes, I too am not liking your English rain. But first I must be looking at my father's van."

I said, "Okay, but make it quick, will

yer. And be careful."

Me, I could see all I wanted from where I was, thank you very much. And let's face it, when you've seen one truck, you've seen them all. More importantly, I wanted to stay where I could keep an eye on the main road for Detective Parry's car. It wouldn't do to have him show up and find us both gone, in which case he'd probably drive straight off again. Then we really would be in trouble.

I reckoned there was near enough a hundred metres of open ground between us and his old man's truck. And stupid as it might sound, I was as nervous as hell all the time he was out there. It didn't help to see him dodging and weaving his way across like every second he was expecting to get shot to pieces in a hail of bullets like they do on telly.

But he made it all right, and I was just starting to relax again when I saw it. The car, I mean. Nosing its way round from the back of Norm's and heading straight for old man Boniface's truck.

What with the headlights and knowing that Jean was out there wandering round on his own in the dark, I suppose I must have panicked. Looking back now, I can't even remember much about it, except that suddenly I'm up and running. I reckon I must have covered those hundred metres in ten seconds flat. Or rather, flat out, on account of the way I travelled the last bit horizontal so as to catch Jean just about knee-height. It must have been the greatest crash-tackle never seen on a rugby pitch. Even old Morgan, our PE teacher, would've been proud of it, I can tell you. Not that I was thinking of him much at the time. Having at least got Jean down flat on the ground, my next concern was keeping him there.

"Crawl!" I hissed.

I'll give him credit for one thing. He didn't ask why. Trouble was, he didn't do much of anything, leastways not so's you'd have noticed.

I don't suppose you've had much experience of dragging some sixty-odd kilos of flat-out Froggy underneath a truck. It isn't easy, believe me. Specially when you're occupying much the same sort of position yourself, and all you can see is headlights coming closer and closer. Not that I could really blame him. It must have come as a bit of a shock being hit from behind like that and suddenly finding yourself wearing a mud pack where your face used to be.

And I suppose if we'd wanted to look on the bright side of it, we were in out of the rain. Though I'd have hardly called lying under old man Boniface's truck "home and dry" if you see what I mean.

It's at times like that you realise why the roads in the mornings are always full of things like squashed hedgehogs and that. I mean, you wonder how come they don't just up and run when they see car headlights hurtling towards them. Well, I'll tell you why. Because they can't. Simple as that. It's like they're hypnotised or something. Their legs turn to whatever it is hedgehogs' legs turn to, and they just stay put until – Splat!

I know – on account of that's precisely what me and Jean did.

Nothing.

We just lay there, staring at the car which was coming straight for us like the driver knew exactly where we were.

It didn't strike me at the time to think much about who was actually driving. Well, I don't suppose it's of much interest to the hedgehog either in the circumstances. Which would help explain why it came as such a shock when the lights suddenly cut out and the car drew up alongside the truck and a door opened to reveal a pair of muddy shoes with trouser legs sticking out of them. I'd have recognised the Gorilla's plates of meat anywhere. Size twenty at least, and they were that close I could have reached out and tied the laces together.

The Gorilla wasn't the only one in the car. Two other pairs of shoes appeared more or less at the same time. One pair obviously belonged to Heavy Breather, judging from the way the car lurched sideways as he climbed out. The third pair was altogether different – brown cowboy-style boots worn over dark blue jeans tucked into the tops. There was only one person I knew wore boots like that. He'd even tried wearing them to school till Mr Butcher had threatened to confiscate them and make him walk home in his socks.

Beaker Simpson!

I couldn't believe it. I let out a groan, which certainly made Jean jump, so that for a split second I thought the others must have heard me, too. In fact they hadn't, and it didn't take long to realise why.

For two such big fellas, Heavy Breather and the Gorilla could sure move fast enough when the mood took them. Even then, it was a moment or two before I sussed what was happening. I suppose you get so used to hearing about things falling off the back of a lorry, it's difficult to fathom when it happens the other way round. But that's what the three of them were up to, right enough. Taking stuff out of the car and loading it into the truck.

You could work it out by watching their feet. Or in Beaker Simpson's case, the lack of feet. Heavy Breather took whatever it was from the car, handed it to the Gorilla, who in turn passed it up to Beaker in the back of the truck. A bit like pass the parcel, except that here the same baddy always ended up with the goodies, if you see what I mean. Four times it happened, and I don't suppose it took them much more than a couple of minutes to do the lot. Beaker stayed a while longer in the truck so that by the time his cowboy boots appeared at ground level again, Heavy Breather and the Gorilla were already in the car, waiting. He barely had time to scramble in beside the Gorilla before they were off, bumping across the car park and out onto the main road.

And do you know something? While all that was going on, not one of them said a word. It was like watching the telly with the sound switched off. Except that this wasn't the telly. This was for real, and I was slap bang in the middle of it – or rather, under it, if you get my meaning.

And that was part of the problem.

Neither of us had the slightest idea what "it" was.

Question: What's small enough to fit in a car but needs to be carried in a truck, light enough for one person to lift but needs a heavy goods vehicle to transport it, and comes in fours in the dark? Answers on a postcard, please.

One thing was certain. All that stuff about Heavy Breather and the Gorilla legging it round the place knocking off people's houses had taken a bigger nose-dive than either Jean or me. Which left yours truly with more than just mud on his face, and a whole lot of explaining to do as and when Detective Parry showed up.

Jean had already decided he couldn't wait that long.

"You must be understanding, Joey," he said scrambling to his feet. "It is necessary for me to know what those men are putting in my father's van."

"Oh sure," I said, remembering what he'd told me about the driver. "I can just see this Michel character standing for that. You said yourself he was in on it. What do you suggest we do? Go up to him and say 'Er, excuse us, Michel. We just happened to be hiding under your truck when we seen these three fellas arrive in a car and start loading stuff in the back – would you mind awfully if we had a look, please?'"

I was angry at myself and I guess it showed.

"As always you are right, Joey," he said. "Michel must not know I am seeing in his van."

"And how are you going to manage that without a key? Climb up the exhaust pipe?"

Jean reached into his pocket.

"Voila!"

Oh, he had a key all right. Several of them, in fact. He said they were the duplicate set he'd used on his cleaning job.

I said I didn't care what they were. He wasn't using them, and that was final.

"I dunno what you call it in France," I said, "but breaking and entering is the same in anybody's language, key or no key."

I was all for handing the whole business over to the police. Specially as Detective Parry should be arriving at any minute. I might have got it wrong about Heavy Breather and the others being the "Grave Robbers" gang, but they were still up to no good. The evidence was somewhere in Michel's van. All the nick-nick brigade had to do was find it, suss out the fellas involved, and put them away for a stretch.

Easy as falling off the back of a lorry, in a manner of speaking. But Jean wasn't having any of it.

"I must be sure," he insisted. "If there is a mistake, there will be bad publicity for my father's company. He will lose much money because people are not wanting to trust him. Then he will be very angry."

"He won't exactly be too chuffed if you wind up dead, either," I said grimly.

Jean shrugged his shoulders.

"This is a risk I am taking, Joey. Because he is my father, you see. I think you would be doing the same for Mrs Edwards, no?"

"And that's another thing," I said changing the subject slightly. "Have you seen the state of the pair of us? Our Mam'll go spare when she sees these clothes. We were supposed to be watching a movie, not taking part in one, remember?"

Jean was getting impatient. I was wasting the one thing we didn't have a lot of – time. Assuming Michel knew what was in the van, he wouldn't want to leave it unattended for longer than necessary. Specially when it seemed just about everybody except me had a key to the thing.

Working on the principle that if you can't beat them, join them, I followed him round to the back of the truck.

There were two doors, huge things about twelve feet high. Even standing on tiptoe I couldn't have reached the handles. Jean must have seen my face. He nudged me and pointed to a much smaller door set into one of the larger ones. It was just big enough for a man to climb through, which would explain how Beaker Simpson had managed to get in and out of the van so easily.

By then, of course, I was shaking like a jelly, so that it was all I could do to hold the torch steady while Jean sussed out the right key. And he wasn't much better. It took him three attempts at least to find the one that fitted.

We clambered in and pulled the door shut behind us.

Chapter 18

I don't suppose you've ever been inside a removal van. When it's full, I mean. It's an odd sensation. A bit like you'd imagine someone's house would be after an earthquake or a teenage party. Beds, tables, chairs, wardrobes – it was all there. Everything but the kitchen sink, and I reckoned we'd even find that if we looked hard enough.

And that was the problem. There was so much stuff, it was difficult to know where to begin. It would take hours to sort through it all. I reckoned we had five, maybe ten minutes at the most.

I could tell Jean was disappointed. He obviously hadn't bargained on finding the van quite so full.

"Well, what do you think?" I said.

He shook his head gloomily.

"I think it is, how you say, like looking for the needle in the haystack."

"Yeah, well, maybe we'll strike lucky," I said, trying to sound more hopeful than I felt. "Where do you want to start, at the back here?"

He shone the torch round.

"I do not think so. It is too obvious. If

the truck is stopped at the Customs, it is the first place they are looking."

Fine. Except that short of doing a quick spot of mountaineering, I couldn't see any way forward. Besides which, a lot of the stuff didn't look too safe. You got the impression that one wrong move could bring an avalanche of antique chairs and potted plants down on your head.

Jean must have guessed what I was thinking.

"There is another way," he said.

"Oh yeah?"

"It is a trick the men use when they are loading the van. Watch."

He shone the torch slowly along the massed wall of assorted furniture, crates and boxes. I still reckoned we'd have more chance getting over the Matterhorn. Jean obviously thought different. He focused in on two tea chests wedged together under a table. There was even more junk piled on top of the table so that we'd have needed ropes and a stepladder at least.

Bending down, Jean started manhandling one of the tea chests. When it was far enough out from under the table, he got down on all fours and squeezed through the gap. He reappeared a few seconds later.

"It is good news, Joey. Come, I will show you."

Daft, you say? Maybe, but then, look at it from my point of view. I mean, for all I knew we were on the verge of solving the crime of the century. At the very least, there was a chance of finally putting one over on Beaker Simpson. So you see, the fact that Jean had the torch and I didn't much fancy getting left on my own in the dark had very little to do with it. Honest.

The trick that Jean had referred to was actually very clever. What Michel had done was put several tables together end to end so's you could crawl underneath them. Sort of like a tunnel. That way, he could pile stuff up on top and all around and no-one would even know the thing was there. Like I said, very clever.

And that wasn't all.

I suppose I must have crawled about halfway down the van on my hands and knees when the tunnel suddenly opened out and there was enough room even to stand up straight and move around. Here were stored more crates and tea chests and a whole variety of suitcases of different shapes and sizes. In the torchlight, they looked just like so many Lego bricks all stacked neatly together.

I was impressed. No wonder it had taken Michel all afternoon to load up. But why go to all that trouble? Jean, as usual, thought he had the answer.

"I think perhaps what we are seeking is hidden here," he said, staring round at the walls of crates and suitcases.

"Yeah? How'd you make that out?"

"It is where the driver will be putting something he does not want others to see."

"Such as?"

He grinned knowingly.

"Perhaps it is his girl's birthday and he wishes to bring her some expensive present. Or maybe at Christmas his friends in England like to smoke and drink a little more than usual, eh, Joey?"

I was getting the picture.

"So he loads up with duty-free stuff, stashes it in his little hidey-hole, and that way the Customs don't get to know about it."

I had to admit it was neat. Not very honest, but neat all the same.

So much, then, for the tricks French truck drivers got up to in their spare time. But I assumed Heavy Breather and the rest were into something a bit more serious than cheap fags and a few bottles of booze. Else why all the secrecy?

The problem was to find that something before someone found us.

I kept thinking of those stupid sums they used to give us at school. You know the sort of thing. If it takes a French truck driver ten minutes to eat three bacon sarnies and drink two mugs of Norm's coffee, how long before he throws up and comes back to his vehicle? Looking round, the answer was always going to be – not long enough. Certainly there wasn't time to do much more than have a quick shuftie and then head off back through the tunnel. No way was I going to risk getting stuck if Michel suddenly decided to take off for the motorway in a hurry. Climbing into the back of a parked truck is one thing. Jumping off the same truck when it's going like the clappers down the M1 is altogether different.

I told Jean as much. Leastways I started to. I stopped when he suddenly grabbed my arm. At the same moment he switched off the torch and we were plunged into darkness.

"What the...?" I began.

"Sshh!"

There are several ways of telling people to sshh. He said it like he meant it –

so I did.

I could feel his mouth close to my ear.

"Sshh," he whispered again. "Listen."

I held my breath, straining to catch whatever it was he'd heard.

At first there was nothing, leastways nothing that I could hear. I thought he must have been imagining it. Understandable, given the state we were both in.

That's when I heard it too. I tried telling myself it was just rain beating on the side of the van or maybe a door creaking somewhere. But no. There it was again. A sort of shuffling noise. Faint but unmistakeable. It was coming from behind us, from down near the back of the truck.

I felt Jean's grip on my arm tighten. I couldn't see his face, but I knew what he was thinking.

He was thinking there was someone else in the truck.

The shuffling sound stopped, started up again, and just as suddenly stopped. This pattern repeated itself a couple more times. In some ways, the periods of silence were worse. Waiting for the sound to begin again, hoping against hope you'd got it all wrong, and then finding out that you hadn't. The tension was unbearable. Specially when it became obvious where the noise was coming from. The person, whoever he was, had to be in the tunnel. We couldn't make out any light, so presumably he was trying to find his way in the dark. That would explain the shuffling sound and the business of starting and stopping. It didn't answer the most important question, however.

I couldn't help it. I put my mouth up to Jean's ear.

"Who?" I breathed.

He didn't answer. It seemed the intruder wasn't the only person working in the dark.

I reckoned it had to be the driver, Michel. I reasoned it this way. First off, it had to be someone who knew about the tunnel and where to find it. With the exception of a handful of Brummie knock-off merchants and a few hundred French truck drivers, that would seem to eliminate most of the world's population just for starters. Secondly, it had to be someone who was already hanging around the place, on account of we hadn't heard any other vehicles arriving. I'd been listening out specially for that, in case Heavy Breather and company had decided to pay a return visit.

So, then, it all pointed to Michel. He

must have come out of Norm's at the last moment and eyeballed the pair of us climbing into the back of his van. That was my theory, anyway. Even so, two points still bothered me. Assuming it was Michel, why didn't he use a torch? Either that, or simply shout that he knew we were there and to come out with our hands up sort of thing, like they do in the movies?

    I got the answers to both questions sooner than expected.

Chapter 19

Whoever had followed us into the truck, one thing was certain. It wasn't Michel. Not unless he could be in two places at once. And how did I know that? Simple. If Michel was in the tunnel, then who was in the cab starting up the engine?

Our engine. Or rather, the engine that drove the van we just happened to be standing in at the time.

I say "standing", but in fact at that precise moment the pair of us were a foot off the ground and treading air. So, it seemed, were most other things in the van, judging from the amount of noise going on. No exaggeration, for a while there it felt and sounded like the whole of civilisation as we knew it was collapsing round our ears. The dark didn't help, of course. And neither did Michel's driving. I reckon he must have hit every bump and pothole going, almost as if he was aiming for them.

I felt like a lottery ball in that plastic contraption they use on the telly. And with all that crashing and banging going on, it was only a matter of time before somebody's number came up.

Not that we actually saw what

happened, you understand. Just heard the crash and the sound of a man's voice crying out suddenly. Sort of "Aargh!" without the "gh!" bit, if you know what I mean.

To be honest, I didn't give much thought to it at the time. I was too busy looking after number one and wondering what our Mam'd say when she found out her precious little Joseph had been hijacked by some maniac of a French truck driver. I didn't know what this Michel bloke was like, but he couldn't be worse than our Mam with her rag out. I just had to hang on in there and hope I was still around when she caught up with him. Which could take some time, judging by the speed Michel got up once he hit the main road. And I do mean hit, believe me. Whatever happened, it seemed we were in for a bumpy ride in more senses than one.

I decided to risk sitting down. Anything was better than trying to stay upright the way Mad Max was driving. I was bruised and battered enough as it was, and besides I needed time to think.

Jean must have had the same idea. I accidentally brushed his hand as I slumped down against a tea chest.

"Sorry," I said automatically.

He didn't answer. It could simply be that with all the noise he hadn't heard me, of course. Either that, or ...

Cautiously, I reached over to where I thought he was sitting. Sure enough, his hand was still there. But the instant we touched, I knew there was something wrong. The position of his hand gave it away – fingers outstretched, palm facing upwards. Instinctively, I went to pull back, but the truck jolted as Michel changed down a gear. Jean's hand closed round my wrist, his fingers locked in a vice-like grip.

Startled, I also breathed a sigh of relief. For a moment there, I'd thought he was dead.

"Jean!" I said. "Jean! You alright?"

"Yes, thank you, Joey. And you?"

His voice came loud and clear from over on the left somewhere.

The hand gripping my wrist was down on the floor to my right.

I froze. I absolutely froze. My face felt clammy and I thought I was going to be sick. I broke out in a cold sweat so that my clothes felt like they were suddenly stuck to me ...

Don't ask me how long I sat like that. Time didn't seem important somehow. All I was conscious of was that hand holding on to me, those steely fingers gripping my wrist. Sure, I could hear a voice – it might even have been my own – but it seemed to be coming from a long way off, like in a dream. I wanted to say something, try to explain. It was useless. The words formed but made no sound.

Someone shone a light in my eyes. A hand was shaking me by the shoulder. Another hand. This one urgent, insistent.

"Joey! Wake up, Joey!"

It had to be our Mam. I told her to go away. It was too early for school, and besides, couldn't she see I was dreaming? The light was hurting my eyes. I tried pushing it away. I couldn't wake up yet. Not while I was still dreaming. Miss Shepherd wouldn't like it. She didn't like essays that ended " … and then I woke up and found it had all been a dream."

Jean never did own up to actually hitting me. If I asked him about it, he would just shrug and look the other way. But I can vaguely remember this sharp stinging sensation on the side of my face and then coming to suddenly. I thought I must have been asleep. But Jean reckoned as it was shock, and I guess he was probably right.

He explained as how he'd got worried when I clammed up all of a sudden and didn't answer him. He'd sussed there was something wrong, but in the confusion had dropped the torch. It had taken him a while to find it again.

"And that was the light I could see, was it?" I said.

He nodded. I didn't let on I'd thought it was our Mam opening the curtains in my bedroom.

"You stare like you are seeing a ghost," he said. "I am shining the torch in your eyes to make you blink."

The word "ghost" brought it all flooding back.

"And … and what about, you know … it?" I stammered.

"The hand? It is real enough. Here," he shone the torch down at the floor beside me, "see for yourself."

It was real enough all right. Fingers and thumb outstretched, the palm turned upwards. Exactly as I remembered it.

I shuddered.

"At first I am not seeing it either," he said. "I think perhaps you have received a bump on the head and cannot move. It is when I am checking for the injury that I see the man's hand gripping your wrist. I guess then what has happened and think maybe you are in shock. Do not worry," he went on quickly, "it is understandable. You think the person is me and then discover it is someone else."

Fine, except that we still didn't know who that someone was. And shining the torch didn't throw much light on the problem. The man's hand was wedged between two packing cases. These and several others must have come dislodged when Michel started off across the car park. Which would account for the crash we'd heard followed by the sound of the man's voice crying out. Presumably the rest of him was sprawled out in the tunnel behind the jumble of cases. It still didn't explain who he was or how come he'd managed to scare me half to death.

Jean thought he knew the answer to the second part at least.

"A person does not need to be conscious for him to grip and hold on to something," he said matter-of-factly. "It is an automatic reaction. I have seen such a thing many times in the American cowboy films. Dead man's grip, I think they are calling it."

I gulped and felt my stomach turn.

"You mean ... you mean you think the

guy's dead?"

It was like waking up from one nightmare and finding yourself slap bang in the middle of another one.

"No," he said quickly. "He is not dead. I feel a pulse when I am taking his hand from your wrist. It was not easy. He has strong fingers and was holding very tightly."

"You don't have to tell me," I said rubbing my wrist where it still hurt. I could feel pins and needles where the blood still wasn't circulating properly. If what Jean had said was true, it was probably a miracle my hand hadn't dropped off.

It was a good couple of minutes before either of us spoke again. It was probably seeing the man's hand again that did it. That, and a sudden realisation of the sheer size of the mess we were in. At one point, I stole a sideways glance at Jean. I was trying to fathom what he made of it all. Not very much, if the expression on his face was anything to go by. He was just sort of sitting there, half-slumped and looking dejected, with his back against a tea chest marked "Fragile – handle with care". Which kind of made nonsense of the way Michel was driving. I assumed we were on the motorway and halfway to France by then.

"Well," I said at last, "you've got to admit it beats going to the cinema."

He looked up slowly and all sort of mournful. A bit like a dog that's done a whoopsie in the wrong place and expects to get told off.

"I am sorry, Joey," he said. "I am not meaning any of this to happen. It is all my fault."

Well that was a start.

"Yeah, well, just so long as you remember to tell that to our Mam when the time comes," I said. "And to our Vicki and Miss Shepherd and Detective Parry and Mrs Lewis," I added, just for good measure. In this sort of situation there was a lot to be said for safety in numbers. Call it insurance, if you like.

My talking about our Mam didn't improve matters. If anything, it made him worse. I reckoned what we needed was a plan of attack. That's what people always do in the movies when they're in trouble. Decide on a plan of attack.

First off, there was the question of supplies. Food, water, that sort of thing. Easy enough. We had none. Not so much as a stick of chewing gum between the pair of us.

The second point took a bit longer to

sort out. What to do about the fella in the tunnel. Obviously we couldn't just leave him there. Apart from anything else, he was blocking our only way of getting to the back of the truck again.

You see, I was reckoning it like this. If we could get back along the tunnel, and if we could open the door from inside, and if Michel stopped doing his racing driver act for long enough, then we might just get away with it.

Jump, I mean.

Okay, so it all sounded a bit iffy, not to mention dangerous. So what? You see fellas jumping out of trains and cars and things every day of the week on telly. Admittedly, most of them wind up dead, but that was likely to happen anyway if Michel or any of his mates got their hands on us.

Thinking of hands made my mind up for me. Anything was better than just sitting around.

"Right," I said, getting to my feet. "You can sit there feeling sorry for yourself if you want to. Me, I want out. And to start with, I want that fella, whoever he is, out of our tunnel."

"Wait, Joey." He stood up. "There should be a light to help us see. It is working from the electrical circuit of the van."

He even knew exactly where to look for the switch, half-hidden as it was behind a large wardrobe. Better still, the thing worked.

Jean switched off the torch.

"Cosy, eh?" he said with a grin.

"Yeah," I said, staring round at the jumble of furniture. "Nothing like a few home comforts."

Chapter 20

They say things look better in the light. Well, it didn't do much for the wino, believe me. But then I suppose anyone who'd had half a dozen cases, not to mention other bits and pieces, bounce off his head was entitled to look pretty sick. The wino probably just looked worse on account of he hadn't looked particularly good to begin with.

Out cold he was an' all. Hardly surprising, given the weight of some of the things we had to move before we could get him out of the tunnel. And that was no easy matter, I can tell you. Wino he might have been. Weed he certainly wasn't. I reckon it took us a good five minutes to get him stretched out on a rug that Jean had put down specially for the purpose.

Exhausted, we knelt there staring at him. The wino's eyes were closed and he had a massive bruise covering his forehead. He obviously hadn't shaved for days, and the stubble round his chin was matted with dried blood from a cut lip. All in all, he looked a mess.

"You sure he's okay?" I said when I'd got my breath back.

Jean put his ear close to the wino's

mouth and listened. After what seemed an age, he straightened up again and nodded.

"He is alive, I am thinking."

Well, that was something. I breathed a sigh of relief.

"But he is not looking good, and I do not like the way he smells," said Jean, wrinkling up his nose. "It would not be pleasant to give him the kiss of life, eh, Joey?"

I wasn't in the mood for jokes. And besides, anyone who'd been even half willing to let our Vicki slobber all over him couldn't be that fussy.

I leaned back, swaying against a tea chest and waited my moment.

"You know who he is, of course, don't you?"

"Yes, I am recognising him from Norm's. He is the smelly one who drinks too much."

"Yeah, well. I've got news for you," I said. "The wino bit's all a front, a disguise."

He obviously didn't believe me.

"It's true," I went on. "I was watching him in the caff. He's no more a wino than you or me. He's an undercover cop."

"An undercover cop? I am not understanding, Joey. You will explain, please."

"A copper," I said. "A policeman. I'm sure of it."

"You mean like Detective Parry?"

I could tell from his voice he still hadn't sussed.

"Yeah," I said, "like Detective Parry. Except that he's in disguise. Which means he must have been on a job."

Jean took a long, hard look at the wino. Then he said slowly,

"It is a very good disguise, Joey. He does not look like a policeman I would ask the way if I were lost."

"That's the whole idea," I said irritably. "If people don't know he's a cop, then they don't suss they're being watched."

"And you think this underclothes policeman is watching us?"

"Course not," I said. "I reckon he was onto Heavy Breather and the others. He obviously knew they were up to something. That's why he followed us into the van. He probably thinks we're part of the gang. Either that, or he reckoned we were a couple of kids up to no good who might be getting in the way. In which case he'd have been hoping to warn us off."

Jean was looking thoughtful.

"Then he will be pleased to know the truth when he recovers, I am thinking."

"I wouldn't bet on it," I said. "First off, he's gonna have a headache the size of a house. Secondly, I don't reckon he bargained on Michel just taking off like that with the three of us in the back. It could mean we've ruined months of work for him."

"But if he is an underclothes policeman as you are saying, Joey, then he will believe us, will he not?"

I shrugged. Another explanation had just struck me. Something I hadn't thought of before.

"Course," I said, "there is also the possibility that he doesn't actually know about us at all."

"But he is following us into the van. You are saying this yourself, Joey."

"Yeah, but that doesn't prove anything," I said. "I reckon we were in here a good few minutes before we heard anyone. That would have given him plenty of time to leg it across from Norm's. In which case, he probably wouldn't have seen us at all."

"Then he will be getting a shock when he is awake," Jean said.

"Yeah," I said grimly. I couldn't help thinking it was no more than he deserved after the shock he'd given me.

"But if he does not know of us, why is he climbing into the truck?"

"Probably for the same reason we did," I said. "To find whatever it was Beaker Simpson hid that your old man's not supposed to know about."

Jean looked up sharply. The penny, or rather the Euro, had obviously dropped at last.

"Then you are thinking the police know of this business with my father's trucks?"

"Beginning to look that way," I said. "Unless you can figure why else some copper ought to be nosing round one of your old fella's vans in the middle of the night."

He obviously couldn't.

"This is serious, Joey," he said.

I didn't know whether to laugh or cry. So I just said "Yeah" and left it at that.

The important thing was to decide what to do next. Discovering the wino had changed everything.

I tried looking on the bright side. Assuming the copper did eventually wake up, it'd help us if we had something to show him. For all we knew, there might even be a reward. I could see it all – interviews, pictures in the paper, the works. I told Jean what I was thinking.

"I take it you haven't noticed anything unusual," I said, staring round at the maze of crates and furniture.

He shook his head.

"There has been too little time. And like you, I do not know what to look for."

"Well, we've certainly got time now," I said, scrambling to my feet. The van had settled to a more or less constant speed that made it easier to keep from falling over. "I don't suppose this Michel character will be stopping anywhere else along the way?"

It was wishful thinking on my part.

"I do not think so," said Jean. "He will want to cross on an early morning ferry."

"Yeah, well, we'll see about that," I said. "As far as I'm concerned, this is one truck that certainly isn't leaving dry land. Leastways not with me on board. So I reckon we'd best start looking."

I peered into one of the tea chests. It seemed to be full of scrunched-up bits of old newspaper. I took one out. It felt surprisingly heavy. Puzzled, I held it out towards Jean.

He shrugged and looked rather sheepish.

"I am sorry, Joey," he said. "It is the policy of my father's company to be careful.

Therefore we are asking our customers to wrap every item that is small in paper. It takes time, but it is to see that nothing is broken."

I unwrapped the package. Sure enough, inside was some kind of fancy tea cup, the sort where you can't get your fingers into the handle properly.

"Great," I muttered, loud enough for him to hear.

It took me nearly ten minutes to work my way through that particular chest. I reckoned there must have been nearly fifty or so cups and saucers and things, all with the same flowery pattern on them. Whoever owned the stuff either drank an awful lot of tea or else they just didn't like washing up. Which all added up to a load of work for me and a big fat zero as far as finding anything unusual went.

It was the same story with Jean. Half an hour and some eight tea chests later, we decided to give it a rest. We slumped down beside the copper, neither of us saying a word. It was obvious we were getting nowhere slowly. I was reminded of something old Ollie Norris often said to me during science lessons. I used to hate copying things out of textbooks, and he knew it.

"Edwards," he'd say, looking over my shoulder, "you'll get a long way in a long time, boy."

Well, it seemed he was right. At this rate, Michel could drive to France and back before we'd checked through everything. There were dozens more crates and boxes, not to mention a whole stack of suitcases piled up against one side of the van.

I was staring at the suitcases, trying hard to remember something, when Jean said,

"Perhaps we should try to wake the policeman again, Joey. If he has, as you say, been watching the gang, then he may know what we are looking for. Three pairs of eyes are better than two, I am thinking."

"Try telling that to Rip Van Winkle there," I said.

The copper was still doing his impression of a British heavyweight boxer – flat on his back and out for the count. All he needed was "Hello Mum" on the soles of his shoes and he could have been on telly.

Seriously though, I was getting worried about him. If anything, he was looking worse than ever. It was cold in the truck, and all that shaking and bumping about wasn't helping. With everything else that was going on, the last thing we wanted was for him to go and snuff it. I didn't fancy our chances of trying to explain that to a judge. Specially not when they discovered our fingerprints all over the body. That's the sort of thing they lock you up for and throw away the key.

I leant forward and gingerly touched the fella's hand. This time there was no reaction, no dead man's grip. The skin felt cold. I moved my hand along his arm. His clothes were damp. I glanced up.

"You reckon we ought to get him out of these wet clothes?" I said.

"You mean to give him another disguise, Joey? Is that wise? When he wakes up, he will not recognise himself. Then no-one knows he is a policeman, not even he."

"Very funny," I said. "Now, are you going to help or just sit there all night taking the mickey?"

He grinned.

"But I do not see how I can help you, Joey. I am only small. Your English policeman is not so small. I am thinking my clothes will not fit him."

"Not your clothes, you daft beggar," I said. "What about the geezer who owns all this stuff?" I peered at the sticky label attached to one of the tea chests. "This Mr

Francis bloke. Surely there must be some of his clobber around the place. What about in those suitcases?"

"It is possible," Jean said.

"Yeah, well, there's only one way to find out," I said.

I picked up the nearest case and laid it flat on the floor of the van. Jean watched anxiously while I undid the clips. It was obviously okay with him so long as we were just looking through Mr Francis's belongings. He was much less happy at the thought of actually using any of them.

I was right about the suitcase containing clothes. Jam-packed full of them it was. Mrs Francis had a particularly natty line in long evening dresses.

"Oh yes, very nice," I said, taking out a specially fancy one with lots of shiny bits round the top. "Just what we need, I'm sure."

"I am thinking perhaps these are being more suitable for your underclothes policeman," said Jean. He was holding up a pair of black lace knickers and a bra. We fell about laughing.

"Dress him up in that lot," I said, "and he'll be arrested for sure."

Jean nodded.

"I do not think it is such a good

disguise," he said. "The dress will be hiding his hairy legs, yes, but I think the hairy chin will be a dead giveaway."

I put the dress down very slowly and stared at him.

"What did you say?"

He looked at me, puzzled. We'd both stopped laughing.

"Go on," I said. "You said something just now. What was it?"

He shrugged.

"I am making a joke about the policeman's legs and the …"

"No, not that. The other thing. The phrase you used."

"Ah, dead giveaway. It is a good phrase to describe the situation, yes? You use it when you are talking to Detective Parry and …"

I snapped the suitcase shut.

"Of course!" I exclaimed. "That's it. I knew there was something." I gave myself a sharp slap on the forehead. "Idiot!"

Puzzled, Jean said, "This phrase 'dead giveaway' has been bothering you, Joey? I did not realise. It is important to you, yes?"

I shook my head.

"It's not what I said that's important. It's something Detective Parry said.

Something he told us about the gang who were knocking off those houses. You remember?"

"The Grave Robbers, yes. How could I not remember? Your Miss Shepherd was very upset. And then you think you are seeing these men in Norm's Caff. It is why you telephone Miss Shepherd. You think perhaps they are going to do another job, as you put it."

"Yeah, yeah, forget all that," I said impatiently. "Think back to what old Parry told us happened when the gang did knock off a house. About them being experts and all that."

I waited. I knew the answer all right, but I wanted him to confirm it. I could see him going over the conversation in his mind. The suitcase with Mrs Francis's clothes lay forgotten on the floor. Changing the copper into some warmer clothing suddenly didn't seem important anymore.

Chapter 21

I'll say this much for Jean. He had a pretty good memory. In fact, he was able to remember what Detective Parry had said almost word for word. I stopped him when he got to the bit that mattered.

"That's right," I said, getting all excited. "He said as how they were organised, they had transport – and they knew exactly what to take. And then when we looked at Miss Shepherd's list, I reckoned they could have put everything into a suitcase, and you said as how there were always lots of people with suitcases at stations an' that, remember?"

He nodded thoughtfully.

The next step was the big one. I knew I was right, but he might still take some convincing. And there was something else. If I was right, Jean's old man could be in a lot more trouble than we'd imagined. You only had to look at the copper stretched out on the floor to realise that. If the police were keeping an eye on the Boniface trucks, it was obvious they suspected something fishy. It was also odds on they'd think Mr Boniface was behind it all – the Mr Big as he's usually known. All of which could come as a nasty shock to Jean.

In fact, I was worrying about nothing.

He'd already guessed what I was leading up to, leastways most of it. All I needed to do was fill in some of the detail.

"It is an interesting idea, Joey," he said when I'd finished.

"Interesting?" I nearly exploded. "It's bleedin' brilliant, I reckon." Specially if they can get away with it. Which they probably have been doing if what old Parry says is right."

What I couldn't fathom was how the likes of Beaker Simpson and the rest had come up with the idea in the first place. And how come I hadn't sussed it earlier.

"Yes, but it does not prove these things are being taken to France in my father's vans," Jean said.

I didn't blame him for being on the defensive. And he was right about nothing being proved. So far, all we had was an idea and a suitcase full of women's clothes.

Correction. Three suitcases full of women's clothes. The next two we opened must have contained the old girl's summer and autumn collections.

At least the fourth case had something a bit more useful. Mr Francis obviously didn't go in for clothes to the same extent as his wife. He must also have been about three sizes smaller than the copper, which didn't help. I picked out a pullover each for Jean and me to wear under our anoraks, and one of those old-fashioned cardigan things with buttons down the front for the copper. Oh, and there was also a baggy woollen sweater for him – the sort you'd imagine Mr Francis doing the garden in.

Choosing the clothes was one thing. Getting the copper to put them on was something else. To begin with, it needed both of us to lift him into a sitting position. Then it was a question of holding him there while Jean struggled to get his arms and head through the correct holes. It was a bit like trying to dress a rag doll. We were there for ages, and even then he finished up with the sweater on back to front.

But at least it meant we could get on with the important business of finding out what was in the rest of those suitcases.

Half an hour later, I wished we hadn't bothered.

I couldn't believe it. Twenty-odd bags and cases between the pair of us, and not even a sniff of anything unusual. I slammed the lid shut on the last case and turned just in time to see Jean doing the same. He looked up and shrugged.

"It was a good idea, Joey," he said, trying hard to hide his disappointment. "Worth a try, I am thinking. But … c'est la vie, as we say in France."

"Sod it, as we say in England," I said. I lashed out at the case, forgetting it was full of files and paper and stuff. The case stayed exactly where it was. My foot felt like it would never walk again. I slumped down on the floor, feeling cold and tired and thoroughly miserable. Jean came and sat beside me. I suppose I should have felt sorry for him, but I was too busy feeling angry at myself. It was the second time I'd got it wrong about Heavy Breather and the others. But this time hurt the most on account of I'd been so sure I was right.

Dejected, I stared round at the jumble of bags and suitcases. Each one had a neat little luggage label with the owners' new address written in block capitals. MR & MRS T. FRANCIS, 14 RUE DE PERIGORD, 6100 CANNES, FRANCE. Jean guessed what I was thinking.

"Do not blame this Mr Francis, Joey," he said quietly. "It is not his fault he has so many things."

"Save your breath," I muttered sulkily. It was just our luck to come up against someone who looked like he was a one-man export business all on his own. "What beats me is where they're going to put all this junk. It'll take them a month just to sort it out."

Jean pointed to a small yellow sticker on one of the cases.

"There is a system," he said. "This colour tells the driver he should put the case in a bedroom when he is unloading." He pointed to another sticker, only red this time, on the leg of a table. "Red is for the dining room. It is like a code – white for the kitchen, blue for the bathroom, green for the garden and so on. It is a service my father offers to his customers to help them with the move," he went on, obviously warming to the subject. "They place the stickers on as they pack and if they draw a plan, he will even arrange for the furniture to be put in the right places. Many people are anxious on the big day for the removal. This way they can arrive at the new house and find their tables and sofas where they are wanting them, with the television plugged in and even their beds made!"

Sounded like a lot of fuss about nothing as far as I was concerned. But then, I'd never moved house in my life so what did I know about it.

"Yeah, well thanks for the lecture. So what do you suggest we do now? Put a green sticker on our heads and pretend to be garden gnomes or something?"

I peeled a yellow sticker from a tea chest and stuck it on the wino's forehead.

"There you are," I said sarcastically, "a draught excluder for the bedroom."

Jean seemed to get the message. We just sat there for a while not saying a word. I wanted a sulk, and when it comes to sulking, I'm one of the world's best. I should be – I had a good teacher in our Vicki. I even pretended not to notice when he crawled over to the pile of cases and started inspecting the coloured stickers.

"Satisfied?" I grunted when he'd sat down again. "Got everything in the right place for our precious Mr and Mrs Francis, have we?"

He didn't answer, which suited me just fine. I went back to sulking and concentrated on trying to block out the drone of the engine which was beginning to give me a headache.

It didn't last – the silence I mean.

"Joey?"

"What?"

"There is something I am not understanding, Joey. About the stickers."

We were back to that again. I shot him one of my looks which said "Give it a rest, will yer" or words to that effect.

"It is as I described it to you, Joey. But …" He paused. I sat waiting for the great pronouncement. It came with all the force of a damp squib on a wet bonfire night. "But there are some cases without stickers."

Earth shattering, wasn't it? I mean, there we were, belting down the motorway in the back of a truck with an unconscious copper and who knew what for company, and all he wanted to do was complete his sticker collection.

"You are not thinking this is perhaps strange, Joey?" he said when I didn't reply.

"That's right," I said savagely. "I don't think it's strange. What I do think is strange is the way you keep going on about it."

"I am sorry, Joey," he said quietly. "I only tell you this because it concerns the suitcases and I am thinking you would like to know."

"Stuff the cases!" I snapped. I bent forward to rub my toes where they were still hurting. "I wouldn't care if I never saw another one as long as I live."

He nodded.

"I understand. You are angry that we

do not find anything. But I think perhaps we do not look closely enough."

I sat up pretty sharpish then.

"If you're saying what I think you're saying, forget it," I said. "I'm not going through that little lot again, and that's final. Okay?"

He nodded again. It was getting so he reminded me of one of those stupid toy dogs you see in the backs of cars.

"It will not be necessary," he said. "I am thinking only of four suitcases. They are …"

"Don't tell me, let me guess. The four without stickers, right?"

This time the nod was accompanied by a grin.

"Wait," he said, "I will show you. Perhaps it is something, perhaps nothing."

He stood up, swaying uncertainly. Michel had obviously never heard of speed limits on a motorway. Equally, whoever had coined the phrase "It's quicker by rail" had never heard of Michel.

I watched while Jean sorted through the cases. He picked out four and put them side by side. He turned towards me, grinning triumphantly.

"Voila!" he exclaimed.

I clapped my hands together slowly in a sort of mock applause.

"Very good, Jean," I said, trying to sound like one of those primary school teachers you hear sometimes. "And tomorrow we'll use the fingers on both hands and count all the way up to ten."

I'll say this for the Froggy. He could take a joke better than a lot of other kids I could mention.

"I think perhaps you make fun of me, Joey. That is good. It tells me you are not still angry."

I grinned sheepishly. It was difficult to stay mad at him for long. And it had been my idea to go through all the suitcases in the first place. There was still one problem, of course. We'd searched the four cases once before and found nothing. Why should it be any different this time round?

Jean held up his hand.

"Wait," he said. "Look at the cases. Tell me what you see that is different about them."

That was easy enough.

"Nothing," I said.

It was true. They were all made of the same brown leathery stuff and looked like they were a set. They also looked fairly new.

Specially in comparison with most of the others. I suppose that's when I began thinking maybe, just maybe, Jean was on to something. Spread among the other cases and these four didn't look anything special. But put the four together …

I stood up slowly and stared down at the cases. Bending forward, I checked the labels. Four cases, four luggage labels – but no stickers. I took my time. We couldn't afford another mistake. The disappointment would be too much. Jean watched patiently while I checked out the other cases. Every one of them had a sticker of some colour or other. I even looked at several tea chests just for good measure. Sure enough, there was a sticker on each one. When I'd finished, he looked at me expectantly. I nodded.

"Okay," I said. "Let's see what we've got here." I knelt down and flicked open the catches on the first case. "Open sesame!"

This time there was no messing about. I tipped the entire contents onto the floor and watched as Jean searched carefully through them. I could have told him straight off he was wasting his time. The case was one I'd checked before. Couple of jumpers, half a dozen shirts, a few pairs of socks, and that was about it. I remembered thinking at the time it had hardly been worth the effort of packing a whole case. Unless of course …

I felt a knot suddenly tighten where my stomach ought to be. I opened my mouth to say something and shut it again. Jean was carefully folding the shirts ready to put them back in the case. He didn't look up but I knew what he was thinking. One down and three to go. The signs weren't good. The suspense was killing me, but I waited till every item was packed and his hand was on the lid. Then, and only then, was I certain.

"Hold it, Jean!" He looked up, startled. "I'll do that."

I grabbed the handle and yanked the case up into the air. For the second time in as many minutes, the contents spilled out onto the floor.

I held out my other hand.

"Borrow your knife?" I said.

It was one of those Swiss Army jobs and had everything. A sort of miniature tool kit you could carry round in your pocket for emergencies. Like now, for instance. I gave him the case to hold while I selected the meanest, sharpest blade I could find. Jean looked on, obviously confused. I didn't let that bother me. It was going to happen anyway, whether he liked it or not.

I showed him how I wanted the case held. Flat, facing upwards, and with the lid open. I think he sussed then, on account of this pained expression that came over his face. Clearly it was going to hurt him a lot more than it was me.

I pushed the tip of the blade into the soft leather lining in the bottom of the case. The three inch blade pierced the lining. I pressed down until the whole blade had disappeared and only the red handle of the knife still showed above the surface. By rights, there should now be three inches of cold, sharp steel poking through the underside of the case.

Jean didn't need telling. He turned the case over. It was just as I'd expected. Smooth, flat, not even so much as a scratch. If you didn't know better, you'd have sworn the knife was one of those trick ones magicians use.

The trick, of course, wasn't in the knife. It was in the suitcase itself.

Chapter 22

Jean peered inside the case. The knife handle was exactly where we'd left it. He gave a long, low whistle.

"Care to do the honours?" I said with a grin.

He bowed and made a sweeping gesture with his hand.

"After you, Joey."

We settled on a compromise. Like a pair of newly-weds cutting their cake, we each took a hold of the knife. Four clean sharp strokes and it was done. What to all intents and purposes was the lining in the bottom of the case lifted out in one piece. Where there should then have been a gaping hole, there was instead a layer of cotton wool. Two layers, in fact. Like you'd wrap expensive prezzies in.

And believe me, there were some expensive-looking prezzies wrapped up in this particular case. Or rather, in Mr and Mrs Francis's case, if you see what I mean. Diamond rings, brooches, gold earrings, silver and gold chains, pearl necklaces, the whole works. I felt rather like Little Jack Horner. Every time I put my hand into the case, I came out with a different plum. With the contents of that one case alone, I reckon we could have started up a respectable little jewellery business, Jean and me.

Well, maybe not that respectable. I mean, you didn't need to be a genius to suss that the stuff was hot. It certainly brought me out in a sweat just looking at it.

I suppose I should have been pleased, and in a way I was. But in lots of ways I wasn't. I was worried. Worried that the copper wouldn't wake up. Worried that he wouldn't believe our story if he did wake up. Worried what Heavy Breather and the gang would do if they found out. Worried what our Mam'd do if she found out.

It got so I even wondered whether to put the stuff back and pretend we'd never seen it.

Jean had other ideas.

He'd already ditched the contents of the second suitcase and was standing waiting. The knife was poised over the lining.

"Sure, why not?" I said.

It was much the same as before. And by the time we'd emptied the third case, the floor roundabout was beginning to resemble Aladdin's cave. Course, it was all right for Aladdin. Quick rub of the lamp, and there was his own friendly genii to help him scarper with the loot. All we had was the original sleeping policeman dressed as a wino and wearing somebody else's cardy. And you could bet your life he'd think it was us who'd rubbed him up the wrong way to begin with.

I wasn't going to bother with the last of the suitcases. We already had more than enough evidence, and besides I was tired. It had been a long day and I wasn't used to travelling. But Jean insisted. And as it turned out, I'm glad he did.

Like I said before, we guessed all the stuff was nicked. But where from? At least the fourth case provided one answer, even if it did come as a bit of a shock at the time.

It was the paintings that gave it away. Two of them there were. Quite small, each about the size of one of them A4 sheets of paper they give you at school when you get an essay to do. I sussed they weren't your average painting-by-numbers jobs from the way they'd been packed. Someone had certainly been to a lot of trouble. There were no frames, of course, but the paintings had been laid flat between sheets of paper and card and then placed in a sort of slim wallet specially designed for the purpose. It was the first thing we found when Jean slit open the bottom of the case.

The odd thing was, neither picture looked particularly valuable. I can't say I even liked them much. All fields and blue sky and nothing much happening. Landscapes Jean said they were, by somebody called Corot.

I stopped what I was doing and looked up.

"Who?" I said.

"Corot," Jean said. "He was a French painter in the nineteenth century, I think. Now his paintings can fetch much money in my country."

"Corot," I said slowly. "And that's the fella who painted these, is it? You're sure of it?"

He shrugged.

"I am not an expert, Joey. I see the name Corot here and that is enough for me. But I do not think the men who are stealing these things would make mistakes."

Neither did I.

"Here, let's have a shuftie," I said, trying hard to keep calm and not making a very good job of it. "Show me where it says the name."

He pointed to the bottom left hand corner in each picture. You almost needed a magnifying glass to see it, but it was there all right.

I couldn't help it. I leapt up and did a little war dance there and then on the spot. Jean looked on, obviously amused at my sudden enthusiasm for French art.

"I take it you are hearing of this name somewhere before, Joey?" he said when I'd calmed down a little.

"Too right, sunshine!"

I fished a piece of paper out of my jeans' pocket and hastily unfolded it. The list of stolen items was a sight more grubby than when Detective Parry had given it to us. Hardly surprising, I suppose, given all that had happened since the morning. Monday morning, that is. I was assuming we were already into Tuesday, but you couldn't be sure. The effects of Michel's driving had been too much even for Jean's shockproof, waterproof and everything else proof watch. It had stopped at ten forty-five.

Seeing the sheet of paper, Jean cottoned on immediately.

"Mon dieu!" he exclaimed. "It is the list that your Miss Shepherd said was missing."

You've probably sussed by now that Jean's English tended to go a bit haywire when he got excited for any reason. This was one occasion when I really didn't mind. We checked the paintings against the descriptions on the list. They matched.

Jean must have read the expression on my face.

"She will be pleased with you, your Miss Shepherd, Joey."

I took both paintings and sat down by one of the tea chests. I was in another world. It was like suddenly nothing else mattered. I had found Miss Shepherd's paintings – and, presumably, the rest of her old girl's stuff as well. Me, Joey Edwards.

The noise from the engine seemed to be fading into the distance. It changed tone. I thought I could hear a woman's voice somewhere, very faint and a long way off. The engine noise ceased altogether as the voice got louder. I closed my eyes and listened, trying to make out the words. The voice was thanking me, telling me what a brave and clever young man I was. I pictured the face, all sort of happy and smiling. And I was pleased. I came over all hot and embarrassed then, so that it was difficult to get the words out that I wanted to say. I think I managed "Ta, Miss," and then there was a jolt and it's like I don't know where I am any more.

I opened my eyes. There was no sign

of Miss Shepherd, and I realised I must have dozed off. One look at Jean kneeling over the unconscious figure on the floor and I wanted to go straight back to sleep again.

"Good morning, Joey."

I waited for the sarky comment. When none came, I felt slightly guilty.

I grunted something to the effect of "Mornin'" and motioned towards the copper.

"How's he doing? Still out cold?"

I knew I was perished. It was a wonder the fella hadn't frozen to death.

Jean straightened up.

"Better, I am thinking."

"Well, I'm glad somebody is," I muttered.

You've probably gathered I'm not at my best in the mornings. This particular morning I felt lousy. I don't suppose I was looking too posh either. Nothing that a hot bath and a good breakfast wouldn't put right, of course. Unfortunately, old man Boniface's trucks didn't come equipped with room service.

I sat there staring at the copper and generally feeling sorry for myself. Jean was right. The fella did give you the impression he was coming round a bit. I just had to hope he'd come round enough to understand what was going on. Though we did have one thing going for us, of course – the jewellery and paintings and stuff we'd found in the suitcases. Except that there weren't any jewels or paintings. Leastways, not so's you'd notice. For a second or two, I panicked. Surely I hadn't dreamed that up as well? Jean assured me I hadn't.

"I am putting everything back in its place," he explained. "It is better that way." He pointed to rows of suitcases. "See, they are just as before."

It was true. There wasn't a thing out of place. And because the four cases were in with so many others, it was impossible to spot that they were in fact a set. Even then, from the outside they looked like four perfectly normal pieces of luggage.

"Any particular reason?" I said.

I mean, it must have taken him a while to get everything stashed away again. And specially since he'd had to do it all on his own on account of my being asleep. Fine, if that's how he wanted to spend his time. Except that I'd thought we were going to use the cases as evidence to clear us with the copper.

"I am thinking this, too, Joey," he said. "But then I wonder what will happen if the underclothes policeman does not wake up in time. It would not be good for us to be caught by Michel with our hands full."

He had a point there. Being nabbed by one or other of the gang would be bad enough. Being nabbed with their loot scattered all round the place didn't bear thinking about. At least now we still had a chance of bluffing our way out of it. And assuming the copper did recover, we could always open up one of the cases again to prove our story.

Jean had thought of a way round that one too.

"When I am packing the cases, I keep a little something to one side," he went on. "For old time's sake."

He grinned and reached into his pocket. What he'd kept, in fact, was a large and expensive-looking gold ring which I recognised from its description on Miss Shepherd's list of stolen property.

So, all we had to do, then, was tell the copper about the cases, show him the ring, and he could check it off against the list. That way, he'd know we weren't having him on and we wouldn't have to leave everything lying about the place.

Clever stuff, eh? But would it work?
That was down to the copper to

decide. All we could do was sit and wait, and hope the bump on his head hadn't affected his judgement. The signs weren't good. Even with both eyes open, he still looked several sandwiches short of a picnic. I was all for making a start on him there and then, but Jean said to wait a bit longer.

It wasn't easy. I'd heard of slow recoveries, but this was ridiculous. I reckoned you could grow grass in less time than it took for him to come round. One thing was for certain. If he'd been in the Flying Squad, they'd have grounded him years ago. Finally, however, he did manage to struggle into a sitting position. Interestingly, he didn't seem particularly surprised to see us or the surroundings. Which could have been good or bad, depending. Either the bump on the head hadn't affected his memory in any way whatsoever, or he'd recently joined the C.I.D. – and become one Completely Idiotic Detective.

Chapter 23

I settled on attack as being the best means of defence.

"You all right now, mister?" I said. The three of us had been sitting staring at one another for a full minute, and it was making me uncomfortable. "Only you had a bit of a bump on yer head see, and me and me mate was sort of wondering …"

He grunted, and the rest of what I had to say was drowned out by the sound of him clearing his throat. I guess he needed a drink. I know I did.

"Sorry, mister," I began again.

He scowled and spat a big gob of phlegm that landed on a rolled-up piece of carpet. I could tell Jean was annoyed, and I didn't reckon Mr and Mrs Francis would be too chuffed if they knew. He shifted position slightly and stared round the lorry.

I watched him anxiously. What if I was wrong and he really was a wino? His eyes lit on the rows of suitcases. I waited for some reaction. There wasn't any. Either he really didn't know about the cases, or he was being clever. I took a chance. I said,

"You a copper, mister? You know, a policeman like?"

At least there was nothing wrong with his hearing. His head came round like it was on a piece of elastic. One look at that face told me we weren't exactly flavour of the month.

I went on hurriedly.

"Only me and me mate here reckon you are, see, on account of we saw you in Norm's and sussed you were on a case and that's why you followed us and now we're all in it together and we want you to know that we're not part of the gang or anything." I paused just long enough to catch my breath but not so's he had a chance of interrupting. "And we're sorry you got hurt but it was nothing to do with us and if you don't believe us we can prove it, can't we, Jean?"

Jean nodded and held up the ring, right on cue.

"And there's plenty more where that came from," I added just for good measure.

I sat back. My mouth felt dry, and it wasn't just from the effects of talking too much. We'd laid our cards on the table. Now it was the copper's turn.

He took his time looking us over. First me, then the ring, then Jean, then me again. You couldn't blame him for being suspicious, but the suspense was awful. Suddenly, it seemed, he made up his mind. His features relaxed, and we got the nearest thing to a smile we'd seen from him.

"Well, now, laddies," he began. His voice was thick and hoarse and unmistakeably Scottish. "So ye ken ah'm a bobby, d'ye?"

I breathed a sigh of relief, and then did a quick translation for Jean's benefit. The copper looked on, obviously puzzled. When I'd finished, he said,

"Diz yer wee friend here nae speak English, then?"

I wanted to say "No, and that makes two of you," but I didn't, of course. Besides which, Jean got there before me.

"I am French," he said in his best English accent. "My name is Jean. Jean Eduarde Claude Boniface."

I thought the copper was going to have a relapse. His mouth fell open and his eyes looked like they were on stalks. The smile had gone completely.

"So you're Lou Boniface's laddie, are ye?" he said slowly.

I jumped in quickly.

"That's right, mister. That's why we're here, see. This is Jean's old man's truck. I'm Joey. Joey Edwards."

I dried up then, and there was a long silence. Sort of like you get in class when the teacher's asked a question and you all sit there looking at the desk and wonder why nobody's saying anything. If you keep it going long enough, of course, someone always breaks. Usually it's the class creep, or maybe the teacher just gives up. This time it was down to the copper.

He cleared his throat noisily.

"Well, Joey," he began. "Ah'll nae say ah'm pleased to be meeting the pair of ye here, but it seems ah ha nae choice." He leaned forward and held out a hand. I hesitated, then told myself I was being silly. We shook hands. He did the same with Jean. "Ma friends call me Jammy," he said.

I didn't suppose for one minute it was his real name, of course. But I took the hint about his friends right enough.

"Hello, Jammy," I said.

"Hallo, Joey."

With the introductions over, it was time to get down to some serious talking. First off, I wanted to know what he was going to do about Michel and getting us out of the truck. Was he carrying a gun, for example? Or maybe he had a radio somewhere that he could use to summon help. I even had the idea he might be bugged. You know, so that cop shops all round the country could see where he was by following a little blip on their radar screens. I didn't mind being a little blip if it meant getting one over on Beaker Simpson and his pals.

"Whoa up there, laddie," Jammy said, holding up his hand. "Ah'm thinking mebbe ye've bin watchin' a mite too much television. This is nae America, ye ken."

In one sense, I was relieved to hear it. The rate Michel was driving, we could have been anywhere.

"And before we go any further," said Jammy, "ah think ye'd best be startin' at the beginning. Ye've nae told me very much yet, and ah'm interested to ken what two wee laddies hae found oot that the whole British polis force cannae fathom."

Chuffed me that did, the idea of being one up on the coppers. And you've got to admit, it was quite a story. Jammy obviously thought so. He didn't say a word all the time I was talking. Neither did Jean, which surprised me on account of it was more his story than mine. At the time, I put it down to the fact that he'd been up all night and was tired and hungry. I wasn't feeling too posh myself, but at least I'd managed forty winks.

And as for Jammy, well, he'd been kipping from the moment we left Brum.

When I finished, Jammy slipped the ring on his finger and sat looking thoughtful. He obviously did a lot of that sort of thing in his job. When he eventually got to his feet, it was quite an effort. The bang on the head had left him weak, and his legs seemed to have forgotten what they were there for. Michel's driving didn't help, of course. Standing up at the best of times wasn't easy. In Jammy's condition, it was positively dangerous.

He did, though, finally make it across to where the suitcases were lined up. Here we go again, I thought. I supposed he'd want to inspect at least one of the dodgy cases. Which meant more unpacking and repacking. I glanced across at Jean. He looked sort of tense and drawn, and I sussed he didn't much fancy the idea either.

As it happened, Jammy didn't want to see inside the cases. He just sort of looked them over and checked out what we'd said about the missing stickers. And that was more or less it. He gave a sort of grunt, turned, and was suddenly catapulted towards us courtesy of Michel's driving. He landed in a heap on the floor and said something unrepeatable. I didn't bother with the translation.

When he'd recovered, he said,

"Well, laddies. It seems ah owe ye ma congratulations. Spotting them there cases were a smart piece o' detective work and no mistake. Ah ken a good few bobbies as 'ud missed 'em."

I felt ten feet tall.

"Thanks, Jammy," I said.

"Och, nae, Joey." He waved a hand in the air. "Tis ma ought to be thanking ye two."

I looked at Jean and grinned. It seemed he'd been right after all – about the ring and that, I mean. And now we had the police believing us, too.

Things were starting to look up.

Chapter 24

In another sense, they had also started to slow down. Or rather the truck had. I'd been so caught up watching Jammy, I hadn't noticed the engine note change. Jammy had, of course. Which was probably another reason for not bothering to check inside the cases. It would also account for his rather abrupt arrival on the floor beside us. Judging by the number of gear changes and the sensation you got of going round corners, I sussed we were probably coming into a town somewhere.

Jammy obviously thought so, too. His spirits lifted and he began cracking jokes and saying things like he had to go down to the sea again, the lonely sea and the sky. At one point, he even did his wino bit and sang at the top of his voice "There'll be bluebirds over the white cliffs of Dover." I was sure Michel would hear him, but Jammy didn't seem bothered. When I didn't join in the chorus, he said, "Och, Joey, ye've nae sole, nae sole," and then fell about laughing.

I couldn't see what was so funny, but I joined in anyway to humour him. Then, just as quickly, the mood changed and he was all serious again.

"Reet, laddies," he said, "time we were putting our heads together, ah reckon. Wha d'ye say?"

For some reason, I was reminded of that Irish joke. You know the one. Why do two Irish policemen always take a dog with them on patrol? Because three heads are better than two, of course.

In fact, it seemed I was wrong. Jammy'd obviously been giving some thought to the subject and had it all worked out. The best of it was, Jean and me got so as we missed all the rough stuff. As Jammy explained it when I asked a question,

"Dinna worry yer wee head aboot the opposition, Joey. That's ma department. Important thing noo is to keep ye both oot of harm's way so's ye'll nae come to any more mischief."

I couldn't have put it better myself.

"Suits me," I said, giving Jean a dig in the ribs at the same time. I didn't want him playing the hero bit and spoiling our chances of getting back home in one piece with a big fat reward. He got the message.

"Me, too," he said quietly.

So now it was all down to the professionals. I listened fascinated as Jammy outlined what he had in mind. The plan was simple enough, based as it was largely on luck and a fair amount of guesswork. Its success also depended on the accuracy of bits and pieces of information that Jammy said he'd picked up from listening to conversations in Norm's. He'd overheard, for example, that Michel was planning to cross from Dover on the eight-thirty ferry. I glanced at Jean, remembering something he'd said earlier. He nodded.

"It is a favourite sailing with my father's drivers," he said. "This way they can sometimes be with their families again by the next day."

This brought us on to another bit of info that Jammy had picked up. It seemed Michel was in the habit of phoning his family in France an hour or so before the boat left, just to let them know everything was okay. Nothing unusual there, I thought. It was only when Jean pointed out that Michel was single and didn't have a family that I began to cotton on.

Apparently, this was also news to Jammy.

"Is that reet now, Jean?" he said, sounding disappointed. He was relying on Michel stopping somewhere so's he could put the first part of his plan into operation. "So if

Mad Max up there disna have a wife and bairns, he'll no be needing to phone then, will he?" Jammy stroked a hand over the stubble on his chin and looked thoughtful. "Unless of course …"

"He's really phoning someone in France who's in the gang," I said quickly, "and that way they know when he's coming and what time to meet him at the other end."

Jammy's eyes lit up like Spaghetti Junction on a foggy night.

"Och, laddy," he exclaimed, slapping the palm of his hand on my back, "yer a genius, a bloomin' genius!"

It's always nice to get a pat on the back. Coming from Jammy, it was more the sort of hammer blow that's liable to knock you into the middle of next week. Specially if you're not expecting it – which I wasn't.

While I was still recovering, Jammy explained the reason for his excitement. It was something Norm had said back there in the caff. Something about asking to be remembered to Michel's family when he phoned them. It seemed another piece of the jigsaw had fallen into place. I can't say I was particularly surprised. I mean, Jammy was only confirming what I'd suspected all along about Norm being one of the gang. He might even be the ringleader. Specially as it was his caff that seemed to be the nerve centre of the whole operation.

Not that it really mattered one way or the other. At the time, Norm and his caff seemed miles away – which they were, of course. We were more concerned with getting Jammy out of the truck so's he could set to work on phase two of his plan. Much depended on where Michel stopped to make his phone call. Jammy was hoping for a garage or maybe a caff somewhere. That would give him more time to make his move.

As Jammy said, the timing was crucial. He might only have a few seconds in which to surprise Michel and put him under arrest. In which case, he didn't want the pair of us around complicating matters and generally getting in the way. So the plan was for us to stay in the van until he gave us the all clear signal. It seemed a reasonable enough suggestion. And after the hours we'd spent in the truck, I was already beginning to feel like part of the furniture, so I reckoned another few minutes wouldn't hurt.

The time for talking was over. Michel could stop at any moment, and we still had to make our way to the back of the truck. Remembering what had happened to Jammy earlier, it wasn't something I was particularly looking forward to.

I needn't have worried. Apart from the cases that had done for Jammy, very little else seemed to have moved, despite Michel's antics behind the wheel. And I suppose it helped to know that there was very definitely some light at the end of the tunnel, so to speak.

Jammy went first, him being in charge and that. I went next, and Jean brought up the rear. I was beginning to worry about Jean. He'd gone very quiet, and I didn't like it when Jean went quiet. It usually meant he was up to something. Trouble, mostly. Which was another reason I was so pleased when Jammy said as how we were to stay in the truck when the time came for him to tackle Michel.

We didn't have long to wait. No sooner were we out of the tunnel than the van suddenly slowed, turned sharply left, and stopped. I looked up at Jammy expectantly. He shrugged and held out a hand. Two fingers were crossed for luck. I braced myself in case Michel took off again, and waited. There was a loud sort of hissing noise from somewhere under the floor near the rear wheels, and then – silence. Jammy uncrossed his fingers.

It's a funny thing, silence. Sort of eerie. Specially when you've just had your ears pounded for hours on end by the noise from some massive great diesel engine. Not to mention all the creaks and groans from inside the van. And after a minute or two when nothing seemed to be happening, I started to panic. I glanced at Jammy. What if he'd got it wrong about the phone call? What if Michel had stopped for some other reason entirely? What if he didn't get down from the cab? What if …

The sound of the cab door slamming shut echoed through the truck. I breathed a sigh of relief. So far so good. Jammy gave us the thumbs up sign. He took a key from his trouser pocket and slipped it into the lock. Then, almost before we realised, he was gone. Despite everything, it seemed, he could still move fast enough when he had to.

I put my ear right up against the door, hoping to catch something of what was going on. It was useless. The one time in the past few hours when I could actually hear if anything was happening – and nothing was.

Jean yanked at my sleeve from behind.

"Joey, Joey!"

I pulled my arm away.

"No, Joey," he said, "this is important."

"Give over, will you," I said irritably. "I'm trying to listen outside."

"No, Joey, don't. There is not time."

After his recent dumb-show act, he'd sure picked a fine time to start making with the verbals. I turned on him.

"What you on about?" I said angrily. "Isn't time for what?"

"For anything. Please, Joey! Do not ask questions. We must hurry."

I remembered the last time he'd said something like that. We were outside Villa Park and he was pleading with me to take him to Norm's Caff. And we all know what happened after that. Now here he was trying it on again, hoping I'd fall for it a second time. No way, I thought. Absolutely no way.

I made a point of standing between him and the door.

"Look, Jean," I said as firmly as I could.

He shook his head.

"I am sorry, Joey. There is no time to talk. It is too dangerous. We must go now!"

He caught hold my arm. I pushed him away.

"Oh yeah?" I said sarcastically. "And

where to exactly? No, don't tell me, let me guess." I jerked a thumb over my shoulder. "Out there, right?"

"But Joey," he began again, "you are not understanding …"

"That's where you're wrong, sunshine," I snapped. "I understand perfectly. I know exactly what you're up to, and I'll tell you now – forget it. Jammy said we were to wait here, and that's what we're doing. Right?"

It was meant as a threat and he knew it.

He clenched his fist and glared at me. I hadn't seen him look quite so mad since that business with Beaker Simpson over our Vicki. I tensed, half-expecting him to rush the door. What he did do was suddenly smash his fist hard against the object nearest him. Which, fortunately for him, just happened to be the padded back of a fireside chair. Anything else, and he'd have probably broken his wrist.

As it was, what with Michel's driving, Jammy gobbing all over the place, and now Jean doing his macho bit, I began to feel sorry for Mr and Mrs Francis and their belongings. Much more of this and they'd be lucky to have anything left in the way of decent furniture.

But that was their problem. Mine was to keep Jean in the van and out of trouble. Thinking maybe he'd calmed down after his bout of fisticuffs with the chair, I tried reasoning with him.

"Listen, Jean," I said, "I know you'd rather be out there sticking the boot into this Michel fella 'cos of what he's done to your old man. But Jammy's right. If we got in the way …"

"You believe him?" Jean suddenly exploded. "You believe what this Jammy tells you, Joey?"

Okay, so maybe I'd got it wrong about him calming down a little. But why the sudden outburst against Jammy? It didn't make sense.

"Course I believe him," I retorted angrily. "Why shouldn't I? Why shouldn't anybody? He's a cop, isn't he?"

There was a pause.

"No, I do not think so, Joey."

He was joking, of course.

"You're joking, of course," I said.

Jean shook his head.

"We do not have time for jokes, I am afraid, Joey."

I stared him straight in the face. He didn't look like he was joking.

"Prove it," I said suddenly. "Go on, prove Jammy's not a copper. And don't say there isn't time," I added quickly. "Make time."

He held up three fingers on his right hand.

"One. He uses my father's nickname. 'So you're Lou Boniface's laddie, are ye?' he says. It is a name used only by very few people. The family, yes, and maybe some drivers who know the reason for it. He can be hearing this name only from Michel, I think. Two. He has a key to open the lorry. You see it yourself just now. When I search him, I am also seeing this key and I think it strange."

I couldn't believe what I was hearing.

"You searched him?" I said. "When? When did you search him? I didn't see you search him."

"When you were sleeping. Three. He has in his pocket a wallet. It contains much money. I count over a hundred of your English pounds. It does not look good with his disguise, I think. Bad men would not believe his story if they discovered so much money."

He had a point. Several, in fact. Any copper working under cover ran the risk of being spotted. The last thing he'd want, then, is something on him that gave the game away. And in Jammy's case, you'd have thought carrying a wallet with a hundred quid in it was asking for trouble. Specially with the likes of Norm and the Gorilla around. It was the kind of mistake you only made once. Your next job was likely to be pushing up daisies in a cemetery somewhere.

Unless, of course, you didn't have to worry about being found out. Which, as far as Jammy was concerned, could mean only one thing. He was in on the whole racket – part of the gang, I mean, along with Norm, Heavy Breather and the rest.

I wanted to be sick. I swallowed hard and stared at the floor.

"Sorry, Jean," I mumbled.

They reckon some people have a sixth sense about right and wrong. Maybe that's what Jean had. With me, it was just a sick sense of having made such a total mess of everything.

Chapter 25

I'll say this for Jean. He wasn't one to rub it in. A shrug of the shoulders, a consoling pat on the back, and it was like nothing had happened. I suppose that's what comes of always being right. You sort of get used to it, like you also get used to other people always being wrong.

Me, I just wanted to curl up in a corner somewhere and die. It didn't help to know that Jammy probably had something similar in mind for the pair of us.

Jean, however, had other ideas.

First off, we had to get out of the truck. I stared dumbly at the small door through which Jammy had vanished, seemingly with any hopes I had for the future. As far as we knew, he hadn't bothered locking it again, and besides, Jean still had his duplicate key. Locked or unlocked, the door wasn't a problem. The problem was what, or rather who, was waiting on the other side. I had this picture of Jammy and Michel standing there, probably less than six feet away, laughing and joking while they decided what to do with us.

Worse still, it was all my fault. I glanced despairingly at the door and then at

Jean. This could be the shortest break for freedom on record.

He must have read my thoughts. Grinning, he said,

"There is another way. Follow me, quickly."

"Another …"

I didn't get to finish. He'd disappeared under the table leading back the way we'd come. In the circumstances, actions obviously spoke louder than words. I caught up with him more or less where we'd started. He was on his knees, hacking away with the Swiss Army knife at the canvas drugget covering the floor. He didn't look up. I crouched down out of his way and waited.

Frankly, I didn't get it. You could see already that the floor was made up of wooden planks which meant, I suppose, that given time, an axe, and the unlikely event that Michel and Jammy suddenly went deaf, we could have smashed our way out. All except for one important detail, that is.

The wooden planks were laid on top of a steel floor that was the underside of the truck. And short of Jean's knife possessing hidden talents as a blow torch, there was no way we'd be getting through that little lot in a hurry.

How did I know about the underside of the truck? Well, for one thing, it stood to reason, didn't it? I mean, you try piling all the furniture and stuff from your house in one room upstairs and see what happens. Most likely bring the house down, it would, I reckon. Secondly, of course, it got so as you noticed little things like that when you were lying flat out under a removal van. Leastways, I had.

Not that I said as much to Jean, of course. I'd already said more than enough as it was, which is how come we were in this mess. So I just bit my tongue and counted off the seconds, hoping against hope he knew what he was doing.

The blade cut another slit in the canvas. Jean reached through, stretching so that his arm was hidden almost up to the shoulder. The suspense was proving too much. I edged forward.

"What is it, Jean?" I hissed, almost falling over him in my anxiety to get a better view. "What you found?"

A couple more strokes with the knife provided the answer. Jean straightened up, pulling and tugging at a flap of canvas.

"Voila!" he said triumphantly. "You like, Joey?"

I liked.

Set in the floor was an inspection hatch, like a trapdoor, just big enough for a man's shoulders to pass through without touching the sides. It was shut, of course, but into one end was set a ring handle, sort of like you get on a soft drinks' can, only bigger.

My heart leapt, I can tell you.

"Nice one, Jean," I said.

He grinned back, and we were friends again.

More to the point, we were still in with a chance. And we had the element of surprise back on our side. Certainly Jammy would get the shock of his life when he found we'd done a bunk. It wouldn't take him long to discover how, of course, but hopefully by then we'd be off and running. We agreed that if the coast was clear and we could stick together, fine. If not, then it was every man for himself.

There wasn't a moment to lose. We shook hands. The right music, searchlights and some barbed wire fencing, and it could have been a scene straight out of the movies. "The Great Truck Escape" or whatever.

Jean switched off the light. We didn't want that showing when we opened the inspection hatch, specially if it was still dark outside. And it might help confuse Michel and Jammy as and when they came looking for us inside the truck. Slow them down a bit maybe, which would give us those few vital extra minutes. Even so, I shuddered a little. I'd forgotten how creepy the place was in the dark. Given the way I was feeling, perhaps "Chicken Run" would have been a better movie title.

    I knelt down and caught hold of the handle. Turning it the way Jean said, I got ready to take the weight of the trapdoor. There was a click, and I felt a sudden pull on my arm. The door dropped several inches. It weighed more than I expected. But at least it was open. I eased it back up a fraction and listened, straining for the slightest sound. Footsteps, voices, anything that might give us a clue as to what was going on outside.

    It smelled cold. I shivered. A car whooshed past nearby, then another. There was also the sound of something you don't hear too often in early morning Birmingham – seagulls! Those were the first sounds of the outside world I'd heard for ages and they were like music to the ears.

    It was time to go time. My heart was racing. Keep calm, I told myself, keep calm. This was very definitely our last chance and

Jean would never forgive me if I blew it now. Specially as we'd both probably wind up dead as a result.

I lowered the trapdoor as far as I could without falling out. Then I let go. It swung backwards and forwards a couple of times. There was a sort of creaking noise but not loud enough so's anyone would notice. The ground underneath showed up as black and shiny wet. Tarmac, I reckoned. Which meant a road or possibly even a car park somewhere. Either way, it was good news.

I went first. One small step for man and all that. It wasn't much of a drop. A metre or so, and my trainers helped muffle the sound.

"Joey?"

It was Jean. He was trying to manoeuvre a suitcase down through the opening and needed a hand. I didn't ask questions. I just took the case and ducked aside so's he had room to jump. We barely had time to close the inspection hatch again. Someone was coming. You could hear his footsteps hurrying along the pavement. Needless to say, we didn't hang around to be introduced. We made a run for it.

Looking back, I suppose we were

lucky. I mean, it's not every day you get fog like that, not even in Brum. Only down on the coast, they don't call it fog. There, it's sea mist. And I certainly missed seeing where I was going all right.

One minute I'm legging it out from under the truck at the speed of light. Next – whoosh! I'm treading air and doing the high jump, long jump and triple jump all at the same time. I'd heard the expression "Look before you leap" but this was ridiculous. No kidding, for a moment there I really believed the Earth was flat and that I'd just run straight off the edge.

I suppose Jean made it to the beach first on account of he was bigger and he also had the suitcase. All I know for a fact is that when I landed in a heap, he was already sprawled face down in what felt like a giant sandpit. Not that I'd have scored much in the way of marks for style or artistic impression, I grant you. But then, there weren't exactly many people around to impress at that time of the morning. Only Jean, and he was too busy spitting sand to notice anyway. Otherwise, I reckoned we had the beach pretty much to ourselves. Leastways the bit of it that Jean hadn't swallowed. Hardly surprising, then, that neither of us felt much like breaking into a quick chorus of "Oh, I do like to be beside the seaside".

Specially with Michel and Jammy standing so close it sounded like they were talking directly over your left shoulder. Which, in a manner of speaking, was true, on account of them being up there on the sea wall and us being some ten feet below them on the beach.

Once I'd recovered from the shock of my first attempt at parachuting without a parachute, I nudged Jean and pointed towards a flight of stone steps that we'd missed on our way down. He spat out another mouthful of sand and nodded. We scuttled across there on all fours, so that anyone out crab-lining and seeing the pair of us would have had a fit. I mean, whoever heard of a five-foot long crab carrying a suitcase?

Huddled together between the angle of wall and steps, I reckoned we'd be safe enough so long as nobody actually came down onto the beach. And certainly neither Michel nor Jammy struck me as the paddling type. Besides, they clearly had more important things on their minds. Specially Michel.

"And you were able to speak with your

friends on the telephone?" he was saying. "You are sure?"

He sounded worried. Not so Jammy.

"Aye, laddie, so dinna concern yerself so much. They'll be along in a few minutes, ye'll see."

I started. I immediately thought of Heavy Breather and company. But surely they were still in Birmingham? It seemed not.

"But how did they know to follow us?" said Michel, taking the words right out of my mouth.

"Och, man, will ye nae relax?" Jammy said irritably. "Ah've told ye before, we're nae amateurs at the game, ye ken. When ah didna come back into the caff after watching yon loading, it meant there was summat wrong. Norm'd have waited a wee while just to be sure like, an' then got in touch wi' the others. 'Twas only a matter o' time before they caught up wi' us."

Michel didn't sound convinced.

"It is a long way to Dover," he said anxiously. "Why are they not catching up with us before now?"

"Aye, well, driving like a maniac in this weather, ye didna gi' them much of a chance now, did ye, laddie?"

When Michel didn't reply, Jammy said,

"Did ye get anything to eat over yon whiles I was on the phone? Ah'm famished."

"These only," Michel said apologetically. "I get them from a machine. The shops are not yet open."

I heard the rustle of paper. My stomach growled with anticipation.

"Aye, well, ah suppose they'll do to be goin' on wi'," said Jammy.

"Ungrateful pig," I muttered.

To add insult to injury, the wrappings from a couple of choccy bars came floating past, quickly followed by several torn pieces of silver foil.

"Wind's getting' up," Jammy commented in between mouthfuls. "Clear some o' this fog away, ah reckon, eh?"

Michel didn't answer. I could hear him pacing up and down beside the truck like he was trying to wear a hole in the ground. Something was bothering him and I didn't reckon it had much to do with the weather forecast. When the footsteps stopped momentarily, I pictured him standing anxiously in front of the rear doors. Serves him right, too, I thought, remembering all that we'd been through on account of his so-called driving.

"Satisfied?" Jammy grunted when

Michel rejoined him. "Ah told ye, they trust me. They'll nae try anything before ah give the signal."

"But you said they have a key …"

"Which is why ah left ma key in the outside o' yon lock. They'll no be able to shift it even if they try."

The sea mist in front of my eyes suddenly turned red. It wasn't often somebody put one over on Joey Edwards as easily as that. I clenched my fists. Yeah, well, I thought, we'll see who gets the last laugh, Jammy whatever-your-name-is. We'll see.

"Are you sure it is him, Monsieur Boniface's boy?" Michel asked.

"Ah'm sure."

"This is bad, very bad. And you say he knows everything?"

"Aye," said Jammy, "and his pal wi' him. Which is why we cannae be taking chances wi' the pair o' them. It's a one-way trip t'bottom o' yon English Channel there for them, ah'm thinking."

A car passed slowly along the road, so that I missed Michel's reply. Not that it mattered. I'd heard all I wanted to hear. Specially as regards Jammy's plans for our future. I gave Jean a nudge.

"Whaddya reckon?" I whispered.

"Chance it?"

He nodded.

"Which way?" I said.

Too late. His reply was lost under a sudden squeal of brakes and the sound of car doors opening and shutting. I counted three at least. With Jammy and Michel, that made for five pairs of eyes and ears. Even with the fog on our side, it was getting so I didn't like the odds. All things considered, then, I reckoned we'd be better off staying put. Leastways for the time being.

With that settled, we turned back to what was happening up on top. Quite a lot, it seemed.

Chapter 26

For all that he'd been pacing up and down, Michel's problem was cold feet. In short, there was no way he was risking driving onto the ferry, he said, with two kids running round loose in the back of his truck. On that point he was definite. He even went so far as to suggest abandoning the whole idea.

"For this journey at least," he said. "It is too dangerous. I think I take the things belonging only to Monsieur and Madame Francis. Another journey maybe, and who knows."

"Leaving us wi' over a hundred grand o' hot property on our hands, ah suppose?" snarled Jammy.

"That is your problem, I think," said Michel. "I am only the driver."

I thought Jammy was going to explode.

"Och, will ye listen to the wee snivelling man!" he exclaimed. "First sign o' trouble and he's away off sayin' 'tis none o' his business, he's only the driver." His voice turned suddenly threatening. "Well, ah'll tell ye this, mon, an' ye listen good. So long as them cases are in the back o' yon truck there, yer working for us, y'understand? Nae for yerself, nae for this Boniface chappie. Yer working for us, an' what we says goes. Reet?"

Put like that, it was difficult to see how Michel could refuse. Needless to say, he didn't. Which was Heavy Breather's cue to join in the discussion. And since wherever he went, the Gorilla was sure to follow, it wasn't difficult to picture the scene up there on the sea wall. Happy little gathering it was an' all.

"Big Mac here's right," said Heavy Breather in that funny way he had of talking.

I started. It was the first time I'd heard Jammy called anything but that. I nudged Jean, remembering the telephone conversation he'd overheard that time between Michel and someone he'd referred to as Big Mac. Another piece of the jigsaw had fallen into place. Jean grinned and gave me one of his "I told you so" looks.

"Or rather, he's right about the cases," Heavy Breather was saying. "Our clients in France are expecting to take delivery of the merchandise later today. It won't look good if we let them down. But I take your point about the, er, two extra packages."

I assumed he was referring to Jean and me.

"It's too risky having them in the back of the truck, even if we tie and gag them."

"Ah had something a mite more permanent in mind," interrupted Big Mac.

"I know," replied Heavy Breather, who gradually seemed to be taking control of matters. "And I daresay you'll get your chance later. Important thing's to make sure the shipment gets off safely. That's Michel's responsibility, and we're not helping by keeping him hanging about like this. What do you say, Michel? We go ahead as planned?"

Michel hesitated.

"What about the boys?" he said.

"They're our problem," Heavy Breather said, clearly relieved now that some of the heat had gone out of the situation and everyone had calmed down a little. "You just concentrate on getting aboard that ferry."

Michel wasn't finished yet.

"The fog is still bad," he said sullenly. "If the boat is not sailing …"

"It'll sail," Heavy Breather interrupted. "Forecast's for a clear day after early morning mist. Heard it on the radio coming down. Should be a pleasant crossing. I almost wish I was coming with you."

I was glad for his sake Heavy Breather had a sense of humour. Something told me he was going to need it.

"Right. Any other questions?" said Heavy Breather. "Okay, then. Mac, you get the kids out here. We'll put them in the car till we decide what to do with them. Beaker, you give him a hand."

I could hear footsteps moving towards the rear of the lorry. Any minute now, I thought, and all hell will be let loose. I tensed, and squirmed as far down behind the steps as possible.

"And Mac, check the cases while you're at it," Heavy Breather called after them. "You never know with kids."

It was like sitting in a bunker waiting for the bomb to go off. I even built up this mental picture of where everyone was at the exact moment. Big Mac inside the truck, Beaker standing by the door, Heavy Breather talking quietly to Michel, with the Gorilla still trying to fathom what he was doing standing on a sea wall in Dover at that time of the morning.

Best of all, though, was the picture I had of Big Mac's face when he discovered the truth. All lovely shades of red and pink it was, to match his purple language. No kidding. I hadn't heard swear words like it since that time old Ollie Norris mixed the wrong chemicals and almost blew himself up along with half the school's science block.

The next few minutes was like listening to one of those radio plays where all they give you are the sound effects and what people are saying and you have to imagine the rest of what's going on. You know the sort of thing …

Sudden burst of loud swearing followed by shouts and the sound of running footsteps. Then,

"What is it, Mac? What's wrong?"

"They've goon, the pair o' them. Scarpered."

Stunned silence, then,

"Mon dieu! C'est impossible!"

"Whaddya mean, gone?"

"What ah said, goon. D'ye nae understand plain English?"

"They can't have. Here, let me have a look. Beaker, give me a hand up."

Scrambling noises accompanied by various grunts and groans. Then,

"Yer wastin' yer time, mon. Ah'm tellin' ye, they're nae in there."

"But you said …"

"Ah ken what ah said reet enough."

"So how come they …"

"Through yon hole in the floor. There's

a door there ah didna ken aboot. Under the canvas."

"And the cases. Did you check the cases?"

"Och , mon, will ye gi' us a moment. Ah'm nae Superman."

"Beaker! Give me a hand down and then get up here and check those cases."

More scrambling noises accompanied by various grunts and groans. A short delay, followed by a muffled cry. Then,

"Beaker! What is it? What's wrong?"

"Only gone and took the lot, ain't they!"

"Whaat?"

"Whaddya mean, the lot? They can't have."

"Well, they bleedin' well 'ave! Look. Stuffed full of clothes. All three of 'em. They must have the other one with them!"

"Oh no."

"Why the little …"

"Sapristi! Que faisons-nous?"

"Well, you can quit bawling for starters. Beaker, get over here. And you, Brains. Right, gentlemen. Thanks to you all, it seems we have a problem. Somewhere out there are two kids with a hundred grand of our property – property that can land us in big trouble if it falls into the wrong hands. I take it you all understand what I am saying. Good. Then I take it you'll also understand if I say that I want those two kids found. Dead or alive it doesn't matter, but I want them found and I want them found with our hundred grand. So, then. Any suggestions?"

Silence.

"Well, that was useful. In which case, listen. They can't have got far, specially not in this fog. And we know they're tired and hungry. Chances are, then, they're wandering round lost somewhere looking for the cop shop. Or, if they're running scared, they may even try and head back to Brum. So, this is what we do. Me and Brains here'll take the car and go back up the road a way towards the ferry terminal. Beaker, you take the beach – and that means all of it, both ends. Mac, you stick with our friend here just so's he doesn't suddenly take it into his head to go riding off into the sunset somewhere. You'll find a bundle of your clothes and things back there in the car. You can get changed in the van. There's a spare phone there as well for you. We can keep in touch on the mobiles. Make sure you keep a careful watch on along the road to the ferry terminal. In the meantime, I'll phone Norm and tell him what's happened in case he needs to make a run for it. There's a pub right opposite the ferry terminal. Meet up in the car park round the back in exactly … thirty minutes. If the kids haven't showed by then, that'll give us time to decide on our next move. One way or another, that stuff's going to France today even if it means we swim across with it! Any questions?"

Pause for shuffling of feet and various clearing of throat noises. Then,

"Right. Thirty minutes it is. And Beaker …"

"Yeah?"

"… try not to fall in and drown yourself, eh?"

Sounds of general movement. Doors being opened and slammed shut. Engines revving up. A car and a van driving off in opposite directions. Then, silence.

Chapter 27

Strange as it may seem, I reckon that was probably my worst moment of all. Worse than that business with the hand in the truck, worse even than finding out the truth about Jammy. No, listening to those fellas driving off like that and knowing what they'd do if they found us – that's what really scared me.

"Dead or alive" Heavy Breather had said, and he'd meant it. More to the point, I believed him. Specially with a hundred thousand pounds at stake. One way or another, an awful lot of people had wound up dead for much less – and I wasn't just talking about in films or on the telly either.

A hundred thousand pounds. I knew what he'd done, of course. Jean, I mean. And when he'd done it. What I didn't know was why exactly. And how come he hadn't said anything. I thought I'd met some cool customers in my time, but he certainly took the biscuit.

I looked down at my hands. They were trembling. My mouth felt dry and parched, and I could taste the salt on my lips. I became conscious of waves lapping gently against the shore somewhere out there in the mist. It was the first time I'd heard them for real and I listened, imagining they were trying to creep in and hide on the beach someplace without anyone knowing. Rather like Jean and me, in fact. Except they didn't have to worry about being found out, of course.

Right on cue, a shower of tiny pebbles came clattering down where Beaker Simpson must have kicked them over the sea wall in a fit of temper. Something told me he wasn't going to enjoy playing the role of beachcomber. Specially when the others were driving round all warm and comfortable.

Scarcely daring to breathe, we flattened ourselves against the wall in the lee of the steps. If Beaker so much as glanced over the side on his way down to the beach, he couldn't fail to see us. We needn't have worried. Judging from the way Beaker stomped down the steps muttering to himself, he was far too narked to notice anything much. I caught a glimpse of him as he slouched off towards the far end of the beach. What with his jeans tucked into cowboy boots, and a brown bomber jacket with the collar turned up, he looked about as much at home as a fish out of water. The odd thing was to see him there at all, of course. I mean, to think we'd travelled all that way from Birmingham only to find ourselves on a beach with Beaker Simpson not fifty metres away and more determined than ever to do us over. It was the sort of thing if you read it in a book you'd just laugh and say it doesn't ever happen like that in real life.

Not that Jean and me were doing much in the way of laughing at the time, of course. But with Beaker temporarily out of the way, it did mean we had a clear run along the beach. Or rather, walk. The state we were in, I don't suppose either of us was actually up to running anywhere. I know I certainly wasn't. Which was another reason for staying away from the road as much as possible in case we were spotted. And at least with the harbour being somewhere nearby, we knew for sure there would be coppers and Customs officials crawling all over the place. It was just a matter of getting there.

I suppose you're wondering how come we didn't just stay put for half an hour or so and wait till we knew for certain the coast was clear, in a manner of speaking. To be honest, I don't reckon the thought even entered our heads. Or if it did, it didn't stay for long. As far as we were concerned, we had thirty minutes to hightail it out of there and find someone in authority who could then round up the gang in one fell swoop. I mean, it was the perfect opportunity. Heavy Breather had even told us where they'd all be. And, of course, there was always the danger that if we stayed where we were, Beaker Simpson would spot us when he came back along the beach. Okay, so we'd been lucky first time round. But there was no telling what a brisk early morning walk by the sea might do to sharpen him up a bit.

We gave it another minute or so, just in case Beaker changed his mind and doubled back. But when he didn't show, we set off in the opposite direction along the beach. The mist was clearing slowly, but so long as we kept in tight against the sea wall it didn't really matter. The important thing was that we couldn't be seen from the road. Walking was easier there an' all, on account of it was more sort of sand and shingle and less of the big pebble stuff like you got lower down the beach.

Even so, it was hardly the day out by the seaside I'd planned for Sharon and me that time I wrote the poem for "Blue Peter". Which reminded me. It was Tuesday. The day whoever had won first prize was due for their trip on the ferry. Oh well, I thought. "C'est la vie", as Jean would say. At least we were still alive. Now it was a question of making sure we stayed that way.

A clock was striking somewhere in the town. We stopped and listened. I counted seven, which seemed about right. There were more cars on the road now. We could see their lights in the distance, picking out the way ahead through the gloom. Sooner or later, we knew, we'd run out of beach and have to take our chances up there with them. We pressed on.

It was slow going. I did offer to carry the suitcase at one point, but Jean said no, he could manage. I didn't argue. Lugging a hundred thousand pounds' worth of stolen property around was a heavy responsibility. This way at least I could keep both hands in my pockets. Neither of us, it seemed, felt much like talking. Too many things to think about, I suppose. Like what was going on at home, for instance. It was the first time I'd stayed out all night and I reckoned as our Mam and Vicki'd be worried sick. Specially our Mam. She'd already have had half the coppers in Brum out looking for us. Problem was, of course, we weren't in Brum. We were in Dover. And the only people looking for us there wanted to play finders keepers.

The blast of a ship's siren split the morning air making me wheel round suddenly. A cross-Channel ferry, looking for all the world like some great white ghost, was nosing its way through the mist towards the harbour. I watched, fascinated, as the huge hull slid effortlessly across the water. It seemed impossible that anything so large could stay afloat, and I felt this tremendous urge to reach out and touch it.

And as I watched, another more familiar shape emerged from out of the swirling mist some hundred metres further back along the beach. Beaker Simpson was walking down by the shoreline and staring out to sea. I should have known. There was no way he could have searched that amount of beach properly in such a short time. It was a few seconds before he saw us, and even then he wasn't quite sure. By the time he had made up his mind, we were already off and running – again.

Straight ahead of us was another set of steps leading up off the beach. We took them at a gallop, half-running, half-falling in the scramble to reach the top. I paused and looked back over the railings. Beaker was obviously finding it hard going on the steeply shelved bank of pebbles, and the cowboy boots weren't helping. It was a case of two steps forward, one step back, so I wasn't surprised when he stopped suddenly and shook his fist angrily in our direction. Another loud blast from the ship's siren drowned out the accompanying verbals, but you didn't have to lip-read to know that he wasn't selling ice creams. I stayed just long enough to wave back and then went haring after Jean.

The Froggy was struggling. Which was understandable given the size of the suitcase and the fact that he hadn't so much as let go of it once since we'd quit the truck. I glanced over my shoulder. Beaker's head was almost level with the top of the steps. We had a good start on him but I wasn't taking any chances.

"Gimme the case!" I yelled.

It wasn't exactly the smoothest changeover you've ever seen, but then this wasn't the Olympic Games either, and at least we didn't drop the thing. We raced on down the pavement. Remember what I said earlier about neither of us being up to running anywhere? Well, don't you believe it! At the rate we were going, I reckon we'd have made Postman Patel look second class. And we certainly made an impression on the old fella who was out taking his alsatian for a walk. He called out something, but needless to say, I didn't answer. My throat felt red-raw, my lungs were hurting and I was ready to drop.

But I could see what were obviously the terminal buildings in the distance and that was enough to keep me going.

Where the road curved away from the sea wall, we cut the corner. I don't suppose the Green Cross Code man would have approved. But then, neither did the driver of the car which just happened to be coming round the corner at the same time. In fact, if he hadn't been so surprised, I reckon the Gorilla might well have aimed straight for us. But he didn't. He swerved instead, and I just caught a fleeting glimpse of Heavy Breather's startled flabby face in the back as we raced past.

Chapter 28

A few yards further on and a notice by the gate read "No Entry". We pretended we couldn't read and darted in past the barrier. Beaker Simpson didn't need to pretend, and a minute or so later he was following us through into the car park. We ducked down between the rows of cars and paused to get our breath back. The sweat was pouring into my eyes and making them sting. I blinked, lifted my head a fraction and peered round. Beaker Simpson was sprawled out over the bonnet of a car a couple of lanes away. He was gulping air and looking for all the world like he was going to be violently sick.

At the far end of the car park, lights showed in the windows of an official-looking building and a huge illuminated sign over the doorways read "Welcome to Dover – Gateway to Europe". Several taxis were drawn up outside. Two men in overalls were unloading equipment from a van parked near the main entrance – one of those outside broadcast vehicles the telly people use when they're filming. This one had the letters BBC down the side. Probably doing an item for the news, I thought. Or maybe somebody famous was around the place. Leastways, there was no sign of Heavy Breather or the Gorilla – yet. But I knew they couldn't be far away.

I waited a couple more minutes then gave Jean the nod and pointed in the direction of the terminal building. We kept low, dodging and weaving in and out of the lines of waiting traffic. Sleepy-looking faces peered curiously out at us through rear windows and from over the tops of steering wheels. An old woman smiled and waved to us from a passing coach. I didn't wave back.

Up ahead, the two men in overalls had finished unloading and were standing waiting by the van. They'd been joined by a tall fella in a sheepskin coat and holding a white plastic cup of something hot. Even at that distance, he looked sort of familiar somehow. A fourth man seemed like he was giving them directions. The van partially blocked my view so that I could just make out the police cap and a uniformed arm pointing.

It was enough. My heart leapt.

I called hoarsely to Jean and pointed. In the excitement, my legs tangled round the suitcase, I stumbled and lost my grip. There was a sharp crack, and a tail-light shattered into fragments of red and amber perspex. A car door opened. Jean snatched up the case.

"Come on!" he yelled.

"Hey you!" a voice began angrily, but we were already four car lengths away and running. The damage had been done, and I wasn't just referring to the tail-light.

I raced ahead of Jean. When I looked up again, the copper was walking away from sheepskin coat and back towards the terminal building. I tried shouting, but at that distance and with so much traffic around it was useless.

Between the last row of cars and the terminal itself was close on a hundred metres of open ground. Bearing in mind what we were carrying, that worked out at about £1000 a metre. I suppose we'd covered the best part of forty thousand quids' worth when I saw them.

Heavy Breather and the Gorilla, I mean.

Coming out of the terminal building right under the "Welcome to Dover" sign. Some welcoming party.

I couldn't believe it. The copper even held the door open for them on his way in. While we'd been busy keeping out of Beaker Simpson's way, they must have parked the car and circled round in the hope of cutting us off.

I skidded to a halt and peered round

desperately. I almost wished I hadn't.

Behind and to our left stood Beaker Simpson, ready, willing and able to block any move we made in that direction. And that wasn't all. Even as I watched, the all too familiar shape of a French removal van pulled in through the entrance on the far side of the compound. Heavy Breather must have called up reinforcements the moment he saw us back there on the road. The enemy was closing in.

We were trapped and Heavy Breather knew it. He also knew that he was taking a chance. Kidnapping in broad daylight is a risky business. The last thing he'd want would be a scene, or anything that would draw attention to what was happening. Which explained the broad smile and the cheery wave of the hand as he slowly made his way towards us.

I suppose that's what gave me the idea. That, and the fact that from where I was I could get a good look proper at sheepskin coat's face as he stood talking to the cameramen. I was still too far away to hear what he was saying, of course, which in a way helped. 'Cos it meant he looked just exactly like he did that time he was announcing the "Blue Peter" competition winners and our Mam went and turned the sound off.

I suppose you're already ahead of me on this one – the day, the place, "Blue Peter", the cameras, the ferry – but put you in my place and what I'd been through and I don't reckon you'd have been thinking too clearly either. Anyway, it seemed like the only ones missing were the prizewinners – which is where Jean and me came in.

There wasn't time to give Jean anything but the briefest of instructions.

"Keep yer gob shut an' follow me. OK?"

He didn't answer but I knew he'd heard me all right.

I kept my eyes fixed firmly on Heavy Breather and the Gorilla. The timing had to be just right. One wrong move and we'd blow it. It was like the final reel in one of those old cowboy films on the telly. You know, when the good guys are surrounded and the hero says, "Hold yer fire, men. Wait till you see the whites of their eyes." Which is fine if your name's John Wayne and you know for a fact the whole U.S. cavalry is about to come charging over the hill to the rescue.

But this wasn't the Wild West, despite what you might think looking at Beaker

Simpson. This was the south coast of England, and we all know they do things differently there.

Heavy Breather and the Gorilla were less than twenty metres away. The Gorilla was on the left as we looked at them. That, at least, was something. It meant if things went to plan, he'd have to clamber round Heavy Breather in order to get to us.

I took a deep breath and started counting, just loud enough so's Jean could hear.

"One … two …"

I saw Heavy Breather's gaze drop momentarily to the suitcase in Jean's grip.

"Three! … Go! Go, go, go!"

I feinted left, then broke to the right. Too late, the Gorilla sussed what was happening. He made a lunge for the suitcase and collided with Heavy Breather. If you've ever seen that film about the "Titanic" hitting an iceberg, you can probably imagine the result. We didn't hang around to pick up survivors. It was a case of women and children first, and since there were no women, that meant us.

We were running side by side. Feet pounded the tarmac behind us. Size twenties and a pair of cowboy boots by the sound of them. Heavy Breather was yelling something at Beaker Simpson, and a sudden sharp squeal of tyres told me Big Mac and Michelin Man weren't far behind.

Sheepskin coat and the two cameramen were still a good fifty metres away. Through the pain, I saw one of the cameramen straighten up. He turned, looked towards us, and panned the camera round on his shoulder in our direction. Sheepskin coat took a step or two forward, smiled, and held out a hand.

"Hello," he began, "you must be …"

"That's right!" I yelled, running straight past the outstretched hand, "and this here's Jean!"

Chapter 29

The next few seconds were a blur of noise and confusion as Jean and me leapt a barrier and made a dash down the ramp towards the car ferry. I do remember the cameraman swinging his camera round so fast to follow us that he caught sheepskin coat a nasty crack on the head and hearing a couple of words that explained where the "blue" in "Blue Peter" came from. I assumed they'd edit that bit out if they ever got round to showing the thing live as it were. Not that we had much chance of seeing the programme if Beaker Simpson had anything to do with it. He was closing on us fast and we were fast running out of ramp.

And you didn't have to be a Mastermind to know that where the ramp ended, the sea began. I know I'd been pretty keen for Sharon and me to see the sea and maybe have a bit of a paddle. But jumping into it fully clothed with an out-of-breath Froggy and a hundred grands' worth of stolen property for company was definitely not part of the plan. And specially not with BBC television filming it for all the world to have a good laugh at.

As it turned out, I was worrying about

nothing, leastways as far as getting wet was concerned, on account of where this particular ramp ended, the ferry began. Huge it was an' all. I don't know quite what I'd been expecting but whatever it was didn't even begin to match up to this particular monster with its huge open doors and massive empty car deck.

      We didn't have to turn round to check on whether Beaker Simpson was still behind us. The clatter his cowboy boots made on the metallic deck echoed right through the whole vessel.

      It's funny how quickly you can find your way round a strange place when you have to. I mean, I'd never been in anything bigger than a bumper boat on the lake at Alton Towers before now, but something told me that the flights of steps leading up from the car deck were our best means of escape. Mind you, we only just made it on account of Jean being weighed down by the suitcase he was carrying. By the time he'd banged and bashed it on just about every other step on the way up, the case was looking a bit the worse for wear. I just had to hope that Miss Shepherd's paintings were still okay, though I guessed some of the other bits and pieces might well qualify for a "Damaged in Transit" label by now.

The steps brought us out into some sort of passenger lounge with rows and rows of empty seats. I dashed ahead of Jean and made straight for the nearest door. The sign read "No Unauthorised Entry". I didn't have a clue what was on the other side, of course. It could have been a broom cupboard for all I knew, but the way I figured it was like this. If we could stay ahead of Beaker for just a few minutes, the place was bound to be crawling with coppers and security guards once sheepskin coat and the rest of the "Blue Peter" team had got their act together. And with us on one side of the door and Beaker Simpson on the other, we'd be able to buy ourselves enough time for the police to get on board and that would be the end of it.

The fact that I didn't have either the time or the breath to explain my thinking to Jean didn't seem to matter. He just followed my lead, which is how come the pair of us ended up in the cockpit or bridge or whatever it is you call the control room of a cross-Channel ferry.

Jean made straight for the control panel with all its knobs and levers and funny dials and things, leaving me to work out how to keep us on one side of the door and

Beaker Simpson on the other. I looked around desperately for something to wedge up against the door, but it was useless. Everything in the room was either bolted to the floor or too big and heavy to move.

I braced myself with my back against the door. Crash! I felt the full force of Beaker Simpson's weight as he shoulder-charged the metal door. His language would have made even a stand-up comedian blush.

I glanced over to where Jean was fiddling with the levers on the control panel. For one horrible second I thought he was trying to start the thing up.

"Jean!" I yelled, bracing myself for Beaker's next battering-ram attack and wondering what was taking the police so long. "What the …"

I didn't get to finish the sentence. There was a sudden crash of breaking glass and a second later the whole door shook and buckled on its hinges. This time Beaker managed to jam his cowboy boot in the opening. That didn't worry me half as much as the sight of the hatchet that Beaker used as a wedge to help keep the door ajar. He must have got it from one of the emergency cabinets which would account for the breaking glass I'd heard.

Any other time and the thought of Beaker Simpson in his cowboy boots with a tomahawk in his hand would have been funny. But this wasn't one of those times. He might not have got the costume quite right but he was certainly on the warpath and it was our scalps he was after.

Beaker was using the hatchet as a lever to force the door open and I could feel my trainers slipping on the metal floor as I strained every muscle in my body to keep him out for those extra seconds before help arrived.

It was no use.

Beaker had the door far enough open now to stick his arm through the gap and he was waving the hatchet around trying to catch me a lucky blow. Lucky for him, that is. Decidedly unlucky for me if he caught me.

"Jean!" I screamed. "Jean! I can't hold him! Get over here will yer!"

This time he didn't ignore me. He turned round and flashed his white teeth in a broad smile. In the outstretched palm of his hand he was balancing a round handle about the size of a billiard ball that he'd unscrewed from the top of one of the control levers. He juggled it up and down a couple of times, testing its weight. Then he drew back his arm and made a practice throw, aiming just above my head and slightly to the right. I guessed what, or rather who, he was aiming at and braced to hurl myself away from the door.

"Wait, Joey!"

He reached into the pocket of his jeans and drew out – our Vicki's scrunchie!

"I am having a much better idea!"

All of a sudden, we'd gone from Cowboys and Indians to David and Goliath. It was a long shot, but the only one we had. I watched as Jean hooked the scrunchie between his fingers and took careful aim with the makeshift catapult. I couldn't help remembering all the times I'd done something similar with bits and pieces of our Vicki's when the elastic had broken or snapped.

"Un … deux … trois!"

I threw myself flat on the deck just as Beaker hurled his whole weight against the door. It crashed open and Beaker half-charged, half-stumbled into the control room.

I don't think he ever saw what hit him. Those hours spent teaching Jean how to play "Killer!" on the dartboard at home hadn't been wasted after all. The shot hit Beaker smack between the eyes and sent him reeling backwards – straight into the arms of the waiting cameraman.

"Gotcha!" said a familiar voice. He might well have swapped his suit and tie for a pair of BBC overalls, but there was no mistaking Detective Sergeant Parry's broad Brummy accent.

Chapter 30

I took another sip from the mug of steaming-hot soup and stared round the room. Detective Parry was perched on the edge of the harbour master's desk, a huge chart of the English Channel on the wall behind him. He'd changed out of the BBC overalls and into a smart grey suit and collar and tie. His jacket hung over the back of a chair. The suitcase lay open on the desk where Detective Parry's oppo, the other "cameraman", was checking off the contents against his lists of stolen property. Jean was there too, of course. He sat huddled in a blanket, talking quietly to Miss Shepherd.

I finished off the soup and put the mug down beside me. Detective Parry looked up from his notebook. He smiled.

"Better now?"

I nodded. He eased himself off the desk.

"We'll just tidy up a few loose ends here and then treat ourselves to a proper breakfast, I reckon." He glanced over towards Miss Shepherd. "What do you say, Julie? Think the lads here have earned it?"

Miss Shepherd laughed.

"I think we all have," she said. "It's

been a long night."

Detective Parry turned to the man sitting behind the desk.

"Mind holding the fort for an hour or so, Dave, while we grab a bite to eat?"

The man waved a hand cheerily over the open suitcase.

"You go ahead, Alan," he said. "I've got more than enough here to keep me busy. Oh, and while you're out, I'll radio the good news back to the lads at the station. Give them something to celebrate."

I looked up.

"What about our Mam?" I began. "She'll be …"

"Your Mam's fine, Joey," interrupted Miss Shepherd. "Just fine. We explained everything to her last night before we came down."

"And we've had someone with her in the house right from the word go," Detective Parry added. "The moment Dave here contacts the station, they'll radio a message through and she can stop worrying. The same goes for Jean's parents. We've already been in touch with the French police as Julie has just been telling him." He paused and smiled knowingly. "Mind you, that's not to say the pair of you won't have a deal of explaining to do when the time comes."

I grinned sheepishly across at Jean.

There was a knock on the office door. A police officer walked in, one of the flat-hat brigade this time. He handed Detective Parry a slip of paper, then stood back, obviously awaiting instructions. Detective Parry read the note, grunted, and dismissed the officer with a polite "Thank you."

"Well, it seems that's that," he said, reaching for his jacket. "All accounted for except one, and I don't expect he'll get far. Now, how's about that …"

"Which one?" I interrupted him.

He glanced up.

"You said there was one you hadn't caught yet. Which one? Heavy Breather?"

Detective Parry stared down at the piece of paper in his hand.

"No," he said slowly. "We've got Mr Malik, or Heavy Breather as you call him. Would you believe, he tried to make a run for it! He didn't get very far, as you can imagine. No, it's the other chap we're still after. The one they call Big Mac."

I started. Detective Parry beckoned me across to a window overlooking the terminal.

"Don't worry," he said, putting a

reassuring arm round my shoulder. "I've got half the Kent police force out there. It's only a matter of time before we find him."

I stared out across the compound. It was true. Every entrance and exit was guarded by at least one jam sandwich, and no-one was getting in or out without being thoroughly checked.

I looked at Detective Parry enquiringly.

"But how?" I began. "I mean, how'd you find out?"

"It's a long story, Joey. I'll explain it over breakfast. But I will say this much. If it hadn't been for you and Jean here, I doubt we'd have caught up with this particular lot in a month of Sundays. You're going to be quite the little celebrities when you get back to Birmingham, I shouldn't wonder." He glanced over his shoulder. "Okay, then. You two ready?"

Jean and Miss Shepherd stood up. As I went to follow them into the corridor, Miss Shepherd stopped me. She put her hand on my arm and squeezed it gently.

"Thank you, Joey," she said quietly. "I won't forget this, you know," and she kissed me lightly on the cheek.

Walking through the passenger terminal, I felt suddenly ten feet tall. All the tiredness had gone from my legs and it was like I was floating on air. I couldn't remember a time when I'd been so happy.

The terminal itself was gradually getting back to normal after all the excitement. The dining room was busy, but we found a table with views over the harbour entrance and sat down. Outside, the mist had cleared totally. It seemed Heavy Breather had been right about that at least. The sea was calm, and showed up every bit as blue and clear and sparkling as I had imagined it.

Detective Parry was true to his word. We had the works – bacon, eggs, sausages, tomatoes, fried bread and lashings of drinks – while he filled in those bits of the story we didn't already know. Like how Norm had finally spilled the beans in order to save his own skin, which was how come the police had been able to set the trap in Dover. The idea of greasy Norm coming clean at last amused me. But how did he know about Jean and me being in the back of the truck?

"He didn't," Detective Parry explained. "No-one did. But one of the drivers we interviewed in the caff said he thought he'd seen two lads messing about in the car park. Putting that with the info Norm gave us, and the removal van seemed the only logical place the pair of you could be. Except of course that by the time we'd worked all that out, you were halfway to Dover – which didn't exactly give us much time, as you can well imagine."

So how come they'd managed to reach Dover ahead of us?

"Police helicopter," Miss Shepherd explained. She smiled across the table at Detective Parry. "Quite exciting it was. I'd never been in a helicopter before."

"Fortunately, the local boys had everything set up and ready by the time we arrived," Detective Parry went on. "The idea was to pick up the truck when it reached the ferry port, then round up the rest of the gang in a separate operation. What we hadn't bargained for was you two making a break for it and heading along the beach. Caused us quite a headache that did once we realised what you were up to."

Puzzled, Jean looked up from his plate.

"But how are you knowing this?" he asked. "We are not seeing any of your policemen on the beach."

Detective Parry laughed.

"Maybe not, Jean," he said. "But one of them saw you."

I had a sudden flash of inspiration.

"The old fella with the dog!" I exclaimed. "The one who called out after us."

Detective Parry nodded.

"That's right," he said. "Though I don't suppose Constable Peters would thank you for calling him 'old'. I'm told he's one of our brightest young bobbies. Only been with the Force a couple of years or so." He pushed back his empty plate and took a swig of coffee. "Of course, we had men posted all round the town, just in case, but it was Peters who spotted you first."

"He deserves a medal," I said. "You couldn't see anything in that mist."

"Ah, but don't forget, Terry, it also meant the gang couldn't see young Peters. Leastways not when it mattered. And even then, we only just had time to switch our men across to here. Believe it or not, we made it literally minutes before you arrived."

"So why the disguises?" I asked, suddenly remembering that business with the two cameramen.

"Stroke of luck, that was," he said with a chuckle. "We wanted something that would enable us to get close to you without arousing suspicion. Fortunately, there's this film team here from some kids' TV programme. Something to do with a competition they've been running."

"'Blue Peter'," I said. "The programme – it's called 'Blue Peter'."

"That's right. You know about it then?"

So I explained about the poetry competition and how I'd been hoping to win the trip on a ferry so's me and Sharon could get to see the sea. When I'd finished, Detective Parry and Miss Shepherd looked at each other across the table, then burst out laughing.

"I'm sorry, Joey," said Miss Shepherd, in between fits of the giggles, "but you've got to admit it sounds almost too good to be true."

Detective Parry obviously agreed.

"Wait till the reporter boys from the papers get to hear about this," he said. "They'll be falling over themselves for the story. I hope you kept a copy of your poem, Joey. I've a feeling you're going to need it!"

I glanced around the dining room. There was hardly a table where someone wasn't reading a newspaper.

"Just think, Jean," I began excitedly. "Tomorrow all these people could be …"

I stopped suddenly. For all his tiredness, Jean was still quick off the mark.

"What is it, Joey?" he said, lowering his glass. "What is wrong?"

Detective Parry and Miss Shepherd had both gone very quiet. They were watching me intently.

Trying hard to keep the tremor out of my voice, I said,

"Table over in the corner. The fella sitting on his own reading the paper. Notice anything?"

Jean peered round cautiously, while I forced myself to sit looking straight ahead through the window. It wasn't easy. When the seconds ticked by and Jean still hadn't replied, I said hoarsely,

"Well?"

Jean shrugged.

"The way he is holding the newspaper, I cannot see him – only his hands."

"That's right," I said quickly. "His hands. Look at his hands!"

This time there was no hesitation.

"Mon dieu!" he exclaimed. "The ring!"

Detective Parry sussed immediately.

"Big Mac?"

I nodded and briefly explained about the ring.

"He must have forgotten about it when he got changed," I said.

Detective Parry placed his serviette on the table and stood up. His eyes narrowed and there was a note of steely determination in his voice.

"Leave this to me," he said.

"No!" I said with a force that took them and me by surprise. "No. This one's mine. I owe him, remember."

"We both do," said Jean quietly.

Detective Parry looked from one to the other of us. I held my breath.

"Okay," he said. "I understand. But I need a minute to get things organised. One minute, all right?"

I nodded.

We watched as he made his way between the tables and out into the foyer. Miss Shepherd glanced down at her watch.

"Time's up," she said. "He's all yours – and be careful!"

I could tell from her tone of voice she thought we were all mad. I grinned across at Jean.

"Ready?"

"Ready."

We stood up and strolled over to where Big Mac was sitting. The heavy gold ring on his finger acted like a magnet. I stared at it long and hard, savouring the moment.

"Hello, Jammy," I said quietly. "Remember us?"

The newspaper lowered slowly.

He looked altogether different from the last time I'd seen him. Smart, well-dressed, clean-shaven even. Any other time and he might have got away with it. For a split second, he believed he still could. But the sudden appearance of Detective Parry and four burly policemen under the sign marked "Exit" soon scotched that idea.

He folded the newspaper and placed it on the table in a gesture of defeat. Only then, it seemed, did he notice the ring. The fingers of his left hand strayed towards it. Our eyes met for the final time.

"That's right, Jammy," I said triumphantly. "The ring. A dead giveaway it was."

Printed in Great Britain
by Amazon